'What the devil is amiss, Serena?' he demanded.

Her breath caught in her chest and speech became painful. But there was no stopping the words from coming out.

'There can be no understanding between us, Wyndham. Every moment I allow you to draw me in, I am compounding my fault.'

'I am trying to help you, not to draw you in.'

'You cannot help me. You, of all people. I am not even supposed to talk to you!'

Wyndham's gaze narrowed. 'Is that your father's command?'

Serena looked him straight in the eyes. 'And my own determination.'

There was silence for a moment. He was holding her gaze, and pain gathered at her heart as she saw the grey eyes grow steely. His voice was no less chilling for its quiet.

'You mentioned once the name of a certain marquis. I do not know what you may have been told to my discredit in this connection. But it wounds me, Serena, that our acquaintance has resulted in you knowing me so little.'

A young woman disappears.
A husband is suspected of murder.
Stirring times for all the neighbourhood in

When the debauched Marquis of Sywell won
Steepwood Abbey years ago at cards, it led to the death
of the then Earl of Yardley. Now he's caused scandal
again by marrying a girl out of his class—and young
enough to be his granddaughter! After being married
only a short time, the Marchioness has disappeared,
leaving no trace of her whereabouts. There is every
expectation that yet more scandals will emerge, though
no one yet knows just how shocking they will be.

The four villages surrounding the Steepwood Abbey
estate are in turmoil, not only with the dire goings-on
at the Abbey, but also with their own affairs. Each
story in **The Steepwood Scandal** follows the mystery
behind the disappearance of the young woman, and the
individual romances of lovers connected in some way
with the intrigue.

Regency Drama
intrigue, mischief...and marriage

AN INNOCENT MISS

Elizabeth Bailey

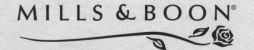

MILLS & BOON®

First published in Great Britain 2001
Harlequin Mills & Boon Limited,
Eton House, 18-24 Paradise Road, Richmond, Surrey TW9 1SR

© Harlequin Books S.A. 2001

Special thanks and acknowledgement are given to Elizabeth Bailey
for her contribution to The Steepwood Scandal series

ISBN 0 263 82843 3

Set in Times Roman 10½ on 12½ pt.
119-0601-61765

Printed and bound in Spain
by Litografia Rosés S.A., Barcelona

Elizabeth Bailey grew up in Malawi, then worked as an actress in British theatre. Her interest in writing grew, at length overtaking acting. Instead, she taught drama, developing a third career as a playright and director. She finds this a fulfilling combination, for each activity fuels the others, firing an incurably romantic imagination. Elizabeth lives in Sussex.

Elizabeth Bailey's second novel in **The Steepwood Scandal**, *The Captain's Return,* follows Annabel Lett's story. Coming soon.

Also look out for Elizabeth Bailey's latest Regency novel, *A Trace of Memory*, in Mills & Boon® Historical Romance™.

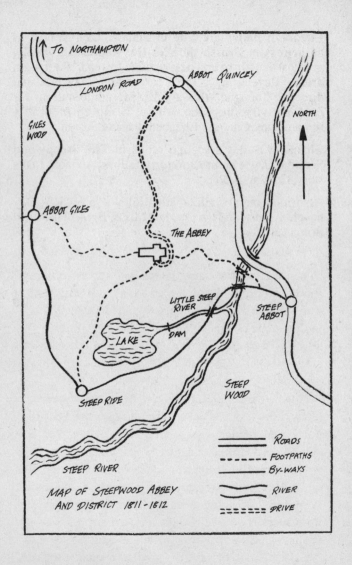

TO NORTHAMPTON

LONDON ROAD

ABBOT QUINCEY

GILES WOOD

NORTH

ABBOT GILES

THE ABBEY

LITTLE STEEP RIVER

STEEP ABBOT

DAM

LAKE

STEEP WOOD

STEEP RIDE

STEEP RIVER

ROADS
FOOTPATHS
BY-WAYS
RIVER
DRIVE

MAP OF STEEPWOOD ABBEY
AND DISTRICT 1811 - 1812

Chapter One

October, 1811

The tick of the large clock on the mantelshelf seemed to grow in volume as the silence lengthened. The younger man looked upon the elder with a growing feeling of chagrin. Could he have misheard? The shock of disbelief held every faculty in check as the grey eyes in Wyndham's lean-cheeked countenance grew cold.

A trifle above average height, his lordship was correctly attired for the occasion in a dark coat and black pantaloons, which overlaid the wiry strength of his slim figure with the elegance which must characterise any adherent to Brummell's decrees of fashion. But no one could accuse George Lyford, Viscount Wyndham, of being a dandy, despite the carefully windswept style of his dark brown hair. He was extravagant neither in dress nor habit, adopting none of the affectations of fashion such as a quizzing glass, and at seven-and-twenty, he had all the weary cynicism of a man of the world.

The last thing he had expected was to succumb to the lure of an artless débutante with a mop of golden curls. Still less had he supposed—though he was not, he hoped, a coxcomb—that his pretensions to the hand of Miss Serena Reeth would have been summarily rejected.

Wyndham knew not what to say to his host. The blow struck at more than his pride, although he must count that deeply wounded.

'Have I understood you correctly, sir?' he uttered at length. 'You refuse my offer?'

Lord Reeth cleared his throat, and gruffly repeated himself. 'My daughter, sir, is not for you.'

'But why?' burst from the frustrated suitor.

Reeth returned no answer, and the Viscount broke away from the elder man's gaze to take an impatient turn about the library. It was a roomy apartment, the tall glass-fronted bookcases causing a trifle of gloom to pervade the place. Or it might have been due to the dank drizzle beyond the windows, uncomfortably dull thus early in October.

Wyndham fetched up at the heavy oak desk, upon which Lord Reeth had caused a candelabrum to be set. In its light, the welter of papers and correspondence bore witness to the Baron's industry. The Viscount turned sharply back upon his host, who had remained by the fireplace, one hand on the mantel.

Lord Reeth made an imposing figure, with that full head of hair of burnished gold, and a Roman nose

that he had refrained—mercifully!—from bequeath-
ing to his lovely daughter. He was of good height,
and had the sense to dress in the sober suiting appropriate to his middle years. He adhered to dark
breeches, though of fashionable cut, and the fit of his
coat was dictated by comfort.

The strong round tones of Reeth's voice served his
oratory well in his chosen field of endeavour—in
which Wyndham had not the smallest interest. He felt
he was grasping at straws as he put the question.

'Can it be that you reject me because I am inactive
in politics?'

His host gave a short bark of laughter. 'If I cared
for that, my dear boy, I dare say I should look in vain
for a suitable *parti* for my girl.'

'And what makes me so unsuitable?' demanded the
Viscount, aggrieved. 'I have no wish to puff off my
consequence, my lord, but I am generally accounted
eligible.'

He knew it to be an understatement. He must have
thought himself a nodcock to imagine for a single
moment that the heir to the Earldom of Kettering,
already master of a handsome fortune, could meet
with a rebuff from a mere baron. But he had met with
one, and it had left him at a loss.

Reeth did not answer him, and Wyndham probed
in another direction. 'Can it be a slur upon my character? Have you been told something to my discredit,
sir? If so, pray enlighten me and allow me an opportunity to—'

'Nothing of the sort!' interrupted Reeth in an impatient tone. Wyndham saw his complexion darken as he came away from the mantel at last, moving to a table to one side upon which reposed a silver tray, heavy with the refreshments his butler had deemed suitable to the occasion. Lord Reeth picked up the decanter.

'Madeira?'

'Thank you, no.'

The Viscount watched his host pour out a glass of the ruby liquid and toss it off. All at once it occurred to him that Reeth was embarrassed. An explanation for his refusal leapt abruptly into Wyndham's mind. Unwelcome, and altogether distressing.

'If those items I have mentioned do not encompass your objections, sir,' he said slowly, 'then I am forced to the conclusion that it is Miss Reeth herself who—'

'Ah, yes!' Reeth suddenly slammed his glass down onto the tray with a force that nearly broke it. He turned quickly towards his guest, his air both apologetic and curiously eager. 'My dear boy, you have hit it! I did not like to say it outright, but I am afraid that my little Serena has indeed turned her face otherwhere.'

Wyndham had supposed that he had run the gamut of emotion during this unpleasant interview. He found himself mistaken, for a sense of bitter hurt rose up, followed immediately by a feeling of outrage.

'I protest I have had no small degree of encouragement from the lady!'

'Possibly you had, sir,' conceded Reeth, thrusting the Roman nose into the air. 'But my daughter, you will allow, is an innocent. She is barely eighteen, you must know.'

'I know, sir. It was that circumstance—'

He broke off, closing his mouth upon what Lord Reeth must find scarcely flattering. It could afford him no satisfaction to know that the Viscount had hesitated to lay his heart at Serena's feet only because she was so very young. He'd had no wish for a bride just out of the schoolroom, and to have fallen victim to Serena's pretty innocence had been an event so much outside his calculations that he had wasted almost the entirety of last Season persuading himself that it had not happened.

Only the summer without the delight of her presence had proved a barren desert. In fact, he had missed her like the devil, and had been wholly unable to enjoy a sojourn with his friends at his hunting-lodge at Bredington, even less a prolonged visit to his ancestral home at Lyford Manor in Derbyshire.

His mother—as might have been expected!—had shrewdly penetrated the reason for his abstraction. Unexpectedly, Lady Kettering had wholeheartedly approved Serena, and encouraged him to declare himself. It had been all the spur Wyndham needed. He had returned to town yesterday, knowing that Reeth must be in residence for the Parliamentary sitting, and presented himself without loss of time in Hanover Square. In vain, it would seem. He had hesitated too long.

Unconsciously echoing his thoughts, Lord Reeth spoke again. 'Had you come to me with this proposal in May or June, my lord, you might have met with a different answer.'

Wyndham set his teeth. 'You are telling me that Miss Reeth favoured me then, but that she has since transferred her affections to another?'

To his surprise, Reeth had occasion once again to clear his throat. What the devil was there in that to embarrass him? Unless he felt his daughter's emotions to be as fickle as did Wyndham himself. He had been so sure of Serena's feeling for him! It was her naïvety in this that had so enchanted him, for had she not worn her heart in those large pansy eyes? Deep brown they were, startling against the mass of gold locks. An oddity which lent a great deal to the sweet seduction of her charm. She was wholly unconscious of it, which had its own attraction.

Yet lovely as she was, she would have held the Viscount's attention but briefly had it not been for the refreshing lack of artifice. He had been at first amused, and then touched, when he had seen her unable to help showing her partiality for him. Or had he been indulging in misplaced vanity?

'She is very young, Wyndham,' said her father excusingly, drawing his attention back. 'It would be surprising if she was not to fancy herself in love with a number of gentlemen before her affections became fixed.'

'No doubt,' said Wyndham coldly. 'But I, my lord, have no wish for a wife whose heart proves thus inconstant.' He strode to the door, and executed a slight bow. 'I will bid you good-day, sir.'

Smarting unbearably, Wyndham left the room, and ran down the stairs in a mood of baffled rage.

From a hidden vantage point above, Miss Serena Reeth watched in bewilderment as Lord Wyndham shrugged on his greatcoat and received his hat from the butler. Had he not then come to make her an offer? The front door closed with finality behind the Viscount, and Serena ran back into the little parlour that had been her nursery and flew to the window.

She was in time to see his lordship climb into his curricle and drive away. Dismayed, she saw the carriage turn the corner of the square. A moment later, the Viscount was lost to sight.

Serena stood frozen at the window, a forlorn figure in a demure muslin morning-gown, with long sleeves ending in a little ruff at the wrists. This feature was repeated about the neck, which dropped into a V-shape, creating a suggestion of décolletage which admirably suited the young lady's slightly buxom form. Her golden hair, loosely confined with a ribbon, fell to her shoulders, and the brown eyes gazed sadly at the rain that drizzled in the empty square.

How could Wyndham have gone without seeing her? She had jumped violently at the knocking on the door—as she had done on each occasion since their return to London, hoping for just this visitor. When she had peeped from the window, her nose pressed to the pane, and had spied him on the steps, her heart had jangled in her chest, racing for all it was worth.

But Cousin Laura had not come to fetch her, as she

usually did when her attendance was required in the saloon, and Serena had at last ventured forth to seek out Lissett.

'His lordship is with Lord Reeth in the book-room, Miss Serena,' the butler had told her, a fatherly gleam in his eye.

Serena had gasped. 'Oh, Lissett, do you think—?'

'Now, now, Miss Serena, do you go and wait in the nursery—I mean, the parlour. Be sure his lordship will send for you, if there's any call for you to have speech with Lord Wyndham.'

But no summons had come from Papa, and Lord Wyndham had left the house—and in so precipitate a fashion! In growing disappointment, Serena came away from the window. She must have been mistaken. The Viscount had not after all offered for her. But what other business could take him to Papa?

The suspense was not to be borne! Serena left the parlour and made her way downstairs to the first floor, heading for her father's library. Outside the door, she was obliged to hesitate before lifting her hand to knock, for her breath seemed to have become tangled up in her throat.

She entered upon the echo of her knock and stood framed in the doorway for a moment, gazing in mute question upon Papa's stern features. Then she saw that Cousin Laura was in the room, had come most probably on the self-same errand.

The duenna was a faded lady of uncertain years, clad in a discreet gown of dove pearl silk made high to the throat, with a lace cap upon her greying hair and a pair of spectacles in her hand with which she was prone to fiddle when stirred. She did so now, apparently undecided whether to keep them on her nose or in her hand even as she swept forward to clasp her charge in her arms.

'Poor dear child! What an escape! And I have ever thought him so very gentleman-like.'

These words cast Serena into bewilderment. She put her cousin aside. 'What can you mean, Cousin Laura? You cannot be speaking of Wyndham!'

Cousin Laura tutted, shoving her spectacles back on her nose as she shut the door. Serena turned to her father, and discovered a portentous frown upon his brow.

'Papa, what is it she means? I had thought Lord Wyndham came to—to—'

'To make you an offer,' finished her father heavily. 'Indeed he did, my child. I am sorry to tell you that I was obliged to refuse my consent.'

Serena's heart plummeted. 'You *refused* him?'

'Dear child, you must not grieve,' came from Cousin Laura, as that lady tried again to enfold her in a fond embrace.

Serena shook her off. 'I cannot believe it. You know, Papa—you *knew* how much I...' Her voice failed and she hunted frantically for her handkerchief.

'Do not think me unfeeling, Serena,' said Reeth, still in that tone of deep solemnity. 'I am palpably to blame. Had I known—had I an inkling of Wyndham's true character, I should never have allowed you to know him well enough to form an attachment.'

But she had formed an attachment! And what in the world did Papa mean by this allusion to his character? Serena blew her nose and sniffed away the rising tears, tucking the handkerchief into her pocket.

'I do not understand you. He is the best of men—the kindest too!'

'He may be as kind as you please, Serena, but as to his being the best of men, you are deceived. As I have been. But you may believe that nothing will induce me to bestow my daughter upon a libertine who runs in the harness of such a man as the Marquis of Sywell!'

Cousin Laura was tutting in the background, but Serena hardly heard her. Wyndham a libertine? It was not possible! Besides, 'I know nothing of the Marquis of Sywell.'

'I should hope not!' uttered Cousin Laura. 'I do not believe a more evil creature lives upon this earth.'

'But who is he?' And what had Wyndham to do with him? But this she did not ask, for a swarm of butterflies danced in her stomach at the question.

She heard Cousin Laura clucking behind her, and was seized with trepidation as Lord Reeth sighed and moved to the fireplace.

'It is not a matter I should ordinarily discuss with you, my child, but I feel bound, under the circumstances, to give you a hint. Sywell, you must understand, has for years been the scourge of the area surrounding his home at Steepwood Abbey. Not a female has been safe since the early nineties when he came to live there. The tales of his debauchery are legion.

I will not distress you with the sum of them, but will say only that every ruinous vice known to man has been Sywell's downfall—and that of every young man whom he has seen fit to corrupt.'

'But not Lord Wyndham!' protested Serena involuntarily. 'Oh, it cannot be true!'

'I think you must accept that it is so. Wyndham owns a hunting-lodge at Bredington, but a mile or two from the infamous Abbey. Indeed, he spent this summer gone there, with a number of cronies, all of whom may be said to be in Sywell's set. You may be sure that the class of female who no doubt frequents Bredington on such occasions is not that with which I could wish my daughter to have acquaintance.'

Serena could bear no more. 'I don't believe it! I will not believe it of him!'

Turning from her father, she fled the room, choking on sobs. Hardly knowing what she did, she ran upstairs, seeking automatically for the solace of her nursery parlour. Slamming the door, she threw herself down upon the day-bed, unable for several bitter moments to control a fit of weeping.

That Wyndham was such a man she could not accept. Papa must be mistaken. How could he know these things? And why had he not known of them last season? It could not be true!

But a seed of doubt lay heavy on her heart. If it was not true, why should Papa have refused his consent? And Wyndham had offered! Despite all, a thrill shot through her at the thought. He had cared for her, after all. How she had despaired when he had not come up to scratch by the end of last season. Summer had been the most miserable time of her life. Or so she had believed. Remembering, she knew that her feelings then were as nothing to those she was now experiencing.

To know that the Viscount wanted to marry her, and to be forced to understand that he was unworthy of the feelings she cherished for him. Oh, this was misery indeed!

The door opened to admit Cousin Laura. Quickly, Serena sat up, dashing away the telltale tears. But it was to no avail. Her duenna came to the day-bed and sat down, possessing herself of Serena's hands.

'My poor girl, I do most sincerely feel for you.'

Serena met her eyes. 'Is it indeed true, cousin?'

Cousin Laura sighed, squeezing the hands she held. 'I am afraid that it is. You see, I happen to know a great deal about the doings of the Marquis of Sywell.'

Serena pulled her hands away, stiffening a little. 'How can that be, cousin?'

'Well, you see, my dear, my father was a clergy-man—'

'The Reverend Geary, yes, I know. What has that to say to anything?'

'I am just going to explain, my dear. I was sent in my girlhood to an academy which was frequented on the whole by daughters of clergymen. It happens that my dearest friend was Miss Lucinda Beattie. Her brother took up a living in Abbot Giles. He has passed on now, poor soul, but Lucinda still lives in a cottage there, and we have always corresponded with regularity, so you see—'

'But what in the world has all this to do with Lord Wyndham?' demanded Serena impatiently.

'Why, Abbot Giles is one of the villages surrounding Steepwood Abbey. So of course Lucinda knows all about the Marquis of Sywell. Indeed, she mentioned in her last letter that Lord Wyndham was known to be staying at Bredington along with several of his intimates. I thought nothing of it at the time, but now that—'

'Then how can you know that Wyndham has had anything to do with this Marquis?' Serena interrupted. 'Merely because he has been in the area—'

'Oh, there can be no doubt of there having been women of ill-repute staying at the hunting-lodge. I am sure it would not be for the first time. Lord Buckworth was certainly there, and he, my dear, besides being Wyndham's boon companion, is a notorious rake!'

'But Wyndham is not a rake. You cannot have heard anyone say that of him, for I certainly have not.'

'No, but we do not know how he conducts himself at Bredington. And Lucinda has frequently spoken of young men attending wild parties at the Abbey.'

Serena got up from the day-bed, crossing to the fireplace where she gripped the mantel until her knuckles shone white. She did not want to believe this! She fought to contain her rising temper as she turned to her duenna.

'For my part, cousin, I should suppose such stories to have been exaggerated. Have you not told me that there are aspects of a gentleman's life about which a wife should not concern herself? You have warned me often enough that I must take care to ignore it if I should find that my husband was engaged upon activities of which I might be supposed to disapprove.'

Cousin Laura drew herself up. 'There is a difference,' she said primly, 'between the peccadilloes to be expected of any normal man, and the depravities of such a person as the Marquis of Sywell and his companions.'

'Well, what is the difference?' asked Serena reasonably. 'Papa will not speak of these things before me, and if you will not tell me either, cousin, then how am I to judge?'

'Oh, dear. Now, Serena, you cannot expect me to—'

'Very well, I shall ask Wyndham himself!'

'Serena! You could not be so dead to all sense of shame as to… Besides, he would say nothing. No gentleman would sully the ears of a delicately nurtured female with such—'

'Well, if the Viscount is so nice in such matters, I shall not believe him capable of—of debauchery,' declared Serena defiantly. 'It must prove a good test if I were to ask him.'

Cousin Laura was moved to leap up from the daybed in great agitation. 'Serena, I utterly forbid you to mention the matter to him! Lord, it sinks me even to think of it! What, will you accuse him of rape and seduction? Will you demand of him whether he has participated in the drunken orgies in which Sywell

indulges? Perhaps you would even speak of the men
and women who cavorted naked in the remains of a
Roman temple in Giles Wood!'

Staring, Serena paled. 'Naked? Orgies?'

'There now, you have made me speak of them!'
Cousin Laura sat down again, tutting and fiddling
with her spectacles in a despairing way. 'Perhaps it
is as well.'

Serena felt her knees shaking under her. Shifting
to a chair to the left of the fireplace, she sank into it,
feeling as if the pit of her stomach had vanished.

'Tell me, pray. If you don't, I shall only imagine
worse.'

'I should hope your imagination was not of an order to conjure up such visions,' said Cousin Laura.
She leaned forward a little, her features creasing into
concern. 'My poor child, you do not know! Sywell
quite scandalised the villages. Every woman employed at the Abbey was either seduced or raped. No
one ever knew whether the women working there
were maids or—to speak plainly—whores. And there
is not a tradesman's daughter around who could count
herself safe from his vile lusts. And all this, mark you,
at drunken parties whose wildness shocked even the
most liberal-minded of gentlemen. Men and women
engaging in the most public displays of wantonness,
in the most degrading postures. I tell you, Serena,
there are no depths to which that man has not sunk.
To say nothing of his reckless gaming. Sywell has
been vilified from the local pulpits on Sundays for
years since. The Reverend William Perceval, I am

told, attacks him regularly from his church at Abbot Quincey.' She paused for breath, eyeing her charge with a distress that Serena had never seen before. 'My poor child, if there is even a suspicion that Wyndham has been involved in these activities, your father did right to reject him.'

Serena was inclined to agree. She felt quite sick, revulsion superseding her distress. She would not have thought it of Wyndham! So kind and teasing as he had always been.

A snatch of memory came into her mind. She was aware of Cousin Laura speaking to her, but she did not hear what was said. For there were his lordship's smiling grey eyes, on the first occasion that he had danced with her.

Lady Sefton had presented him to her at Almacks, and they had stood up together for two country dances. Serena had been too shy to converse with him at first as they came together in the movement of the dance.

'It is customary, Miss Reeth, to exchange a word or two with your partner upon these occasions.'

Serena had looked up and found those grey eyes teasing and warm. She had broken into laughter.

'Well, but I cannot think what to say to you, sir!'

'Come, come, Miss Reeth,' had said Wyndham gently. 'And you the daughter of a noted politician? Surely you can enlighten me on some shrewd governmental move.'

'I should think you know much more about such

things than I, my lord,' Serena had answered candidly.

'I, ma'am? But I am merely a dandy, you know. One of these worthless fribbles who follow Brummell.'

Serena had smiled at this sally. 'I cannot believe that you would follow anyone. And I do not think you are a dandy.'

'You flatter me, Miss Reeth.'

'Oh, no. I admire you very much, sir, but I would not flatter you.'

She had then blushed at the forwardness of her own remark. To her relief, however, the Viscount had laughed.

'But you are delightful, ma'am! I shall certainly sue for a dance another night.'

And he had done so, on several occasions. Serena had found him so comfortable to talk to, for he never scolded, however outspoken she became. And she was afraid that she had been outspoken. But Wyndham, so far from disapproving of her, had elected to enjoy her frankness. Not that she intended to speak so candidly, but she could not seem to help herself. She said whatever came into her head. She knew it to be her besetting sin, and had begged Wyndham not to encourage it.

'My dear Miss Reeth, you must hold me excused,' he had said lightly. 'I cannot be expected to discourage what gives me so much pleasure.'

'But it shouldn't do so, sir. You ought to be excessively displeased with me for the things I say.'

'Upon whose authority?'

'Cousin Laura's.'

'I beg Cousin Laura's pardon, but I cannot sub-scribe to her notions. I pray you will abate not one jot of your refreshing candour!'

Yet Serena doubted whether this large-mindedness would extend to her asking him impertinent questions about his gentlemanly excesses. Cousin Laura was right. She could not ask him. Indeed, she had no wish to do so.

Having spent the better part of the night fighting intrusive memories, Serena determined that she must spare no pains to suppress that *tendre* which she had foolishly allowed herself to feel for my lord Wyndham.

This determination proved more difficult than Serena had bargained for. When she made it, she had thought, in a nebulous way, that Wyndham could never come in her way again. This, she realised on Friday evening, had been foolish.

Not that she would have expected him to be present at the dull party given by one of the political hostesses in Papa's circle. But no sooner did she catch sight of the Viscount at a distance than she recollected that Lady Camelford was a noted society dame as well as the wife of one of Lord Reeth's associates in the government.

The thought passed swiftly, for the consciousness of his lordship's presence ousted every consideration but the desperate need to avoid any sort of confrontation with him. He was looking as elegant as ever, in knee-breeches of cream and a smart blue coat, his neckcloth an intricate arrangement that baffled description. Serena longed for his smile, but knew if she was obliged to speak to him, she would inevitably say the wrong thing. Yet she could not help glancing in his direction—all too frequently.

She was addressed by any number of people, but she was sure she answered them quite at random. Her pulses ran chaotically, and she was obliged to dwell upon the lurid tales that had come from Cousin Laura's lips before she could bring her unruly yearnings under control.

In vain! She had succeeded in exchanging a couple of sensible words with the Honourable Mr Camelford, the son of the house. But just as he moved aside, she found herself face to face with Wyndham.

Serena could not utter a word. His eyes were cold steel, and a sensation of strong emotion emanated from him, washing over her in a wave. Serena shrivelled inside, and a hot flush of distress spread upwards through her veins. Her vision blurred a trifle, and she saw the Viscount's expression change as she quickly looked away.

'Excuse me, my lord.' A husky whisper only.

She whisked about, plunging swiftly among the knots of chattering guests. She thought she heard him call her name, but the tone was so low that she might have been mistaken.

Serena sought instinctively for Cousin Laura, who had, as was her invariable practice, effaced herself among the chaperones. But she emerged as soon as she saw her charge coming towards her, and Serena knew that this presence at her side must secure her from any attempt by Wyndham to accost her.

Not that he had any idea of accosting her! Indeed, Serena believed that he pointedly ignored her. Whenever she dared to look for him, he was certainly not looking her way. The evening became interminable, and Serena developed a headache.

She was glad to retire relatively early to bed, sped on by her duenna's recommendation to forget all about the Viscount. So far from doing so, Serena found herself beset by far too fond memories of the past. Yet each culminated in the horrid image of Wyndham's cold glance on Friday night. By Tuesday, Serena was ready to scream. She must do something to distract herself, or she would go mad.

Hitting upon the idea of finding herself an interesting novel to read, she ventured into Piccadilly with Cousin Laura, and entered Hatchards circulating library. After a pleasant quarter of an hour browsing along the shelves, she was rewarded at last by discovering a novel of which she had heard good report. It was by a new author, and had been published earlier that year.

Serena opened the first volume at random and ran her eyes down the page. She liked what she read, and looked up with the intention of picking up the other two volumes, only to find herself gazing directly into the face that had been haunting her thoughts.

'Well met, Miss Reeth,' said Wyndham drily.

Chapter Two

Serena promptly dropped the book she was holding. Wyndham bent to pick it up for her, noting as he handed it back that her fingers were trembling. She was evidently flustered, for she almost snatched the thing from him, and her eyes flew in every direction as if she sought to escape his gaze.

'Th-thank you, sir,' she uttered breathlessly, and relapsed into silence.

Wyndham tried in vain to suppress the anger he still felt at her perfidy. When he had run into her at the Camelford house, his rage had welled. It had been no surprise to find her conscious and confused. But the abrupt evidence of distress had jerked him out of his own emotions. Then she had turned away, giving him no opportunity to probe the oddity.

The remembrance of the altogether different reception which he had grown accustomed to receive from her had gnawed at him since. It had afforded him no small degree of satisfaction to see the pansy eyes light up at his approach, and the lovely features break into that enchanting smile. It had been the very look which had attracted him when he had first seen her among last Season's fresh crop of débutantes. She had been looking about her with frank enjoyment, and with none of the studied indifference which characterised so many of the young females drilled into conformity by their determined mamas.

When the Viscount had engineered an introduction, he had been obliged to coax her out of her initial shyness. But once Serena had begun to relax, she had astonished him by confiding to him her pleasure in having been singled out by so fashionable and important a member of the *beau monde*. If he had at first thought her guilty of a revolting display of sycophancy, he had been speedily brought to realise that Serena was far too naïve to have any thought of flattery. By the time she had blurted out a series of remarks of similar candour concerning others of his world—and not nearly as complimentary!— Wyndham was in a ripple of amusement.

Serena confided to him that she thought far too many matrons looked disgracefully fat in the fashionable high waists; that she had seen the Regent and thought him a roly-poly fellow; that the patronesses of Almacks were all proud ladies and it was very difficult to be obliged to conciliate them; and that although she knew Mr Brummell's approval was essential, she was in a quake lest he should speak to her, 'For I am bound to say something dreadful to him and disgrace myself.' She had then recollected that the Viscount was an acquaintance of Brummell, and had blushed adorably, saying in a conscience-stricken way, 'Oh, dear, what have I said? Am I already disgraced, sir? Will you betray me to him?'

Wyndham had reassured her, but had been unable to keep from laughing. His artless companion had demanded the reason, and he had readily informed her that so far from disgracing herself, she had succeeded in doing what no other female had done by chasing away the jaded boredom of his existence.

'Well, I cannot imagine how I should have done that,' she had said, looking at him with so much puzzlement as had instantly overset him again.

His acquaintance with her had blossomed, for he had sought her out with more frequency than he had intended until it had been borne in upon him that he was raising expectations which he did not know whether he was ready to fulfil. That had led him to shilly-shally in a fashion that appeared now to have lost her to him. He had not known how bitterly he must repent it when he was greeted by her in a manner so unlike that which had been his downfall.

She was looking delightful in a gown of jaconet with a neat blue spencer atop that enhanced the allure of her figure. And she was blushing furiously, her eyes now fixed upon the volume held tightly between her gloved fingers. On impulse, Wyndham reached out and took it from her, turning it over to find the title.

'So you have succumbed to the dictates of fashion,' he remarked coolly. 'An apt choice, I think.'

He looked up to find her eyes upon him, an expression in them compound of alarm and despondency. Wyndham could not withstand a feeling of compassion. 'Don't look so dismayed! If I have understood your honoured father, you have acted with both sense and sensibility.'

'I fear not, sir. I have too much of one, and not enough of the other.'

A slight smile accompanied the words, and in her eyes an echo of that shy sweetness of which he had grown all too fond. Hurt consumed him, and Wyndham was conscious of an urgent desire to demand of her what she meant by rejecting him.

'I believe you are not alone,' he said coldly, returning the book to her. 'Most females demonstrate sensibility above sense. Or did you mean it the other way about?'

The coolness of his tone struck Serena to the heart. Without thinking, she uttered the chaos of her mind. 'Oh, don't speak to me so, for I cannot bear it! Pray forgive me, sir. No, I don't mean that! But I would never…it was not by any will of mine that—but I must not say so!'

'But you have said so,' the Viscount put in swiftly. 'What does it mean, Serena?'

She felt herself grow hot. How in the world could she answer him? 'Oh, how very difficult this is!'

Wyndham saw her fingers tighten upon the book, and was seized with the conviction that Lord Reeth had fabricated his excuse. Serena was not behaving like a maiden confronted by a man whom she could no longer like! His voice softened.

'Come, Miss Reeth. You were not wont to be so tongue-tied with me.' He smiled teasingly. 'Quite the opposite.'

The smile was almost too much for Serena to bear. Her candid gaze searched his face, and she was no longer mistress of her tongue.

'Is it true that you own a hunting-lodge close to an Abbey? Steepwood, is it not?'

Considerably taken aback, Wyndham frowned. 'I do, yes. It is situated in a place called Steep Wood, and it is indeed a mile or two from Steepwood Abbey.'

Serena clutched the volume between her hands as if to draw support from it. 'Were you—were you there last summer? With Lord Buckworth and—and others?'

His frown deepened. 'I was. What of it? I invariably spend the summer months there.'

'You have done so for some years then,' she said in a blank tone, and drew back a step or two, away from him.

Astonished both by her manner and the line of questioning, Wyndham's tone became curt. 'Why do you ask, Miss Reeth?'

Had he but known it, the abrupt manner of his answer served only to convince Serena that he had something to hide. Her unruly tongue betrayed her.

'You must know why I ask it!' Recollecting herself, she looked away and back again, stammering in her haste to unsay the words. 'I b-beg your pardon, s-sir. I d-did not m-mean— I should not have— Oh, why did you speak to me at all?' she finished despairingly.

Wyndham was by now thoroughly bemused by the rapid contradictions of her attitude. But they could not be ignored!

'What the devil is amiss, Serena? I am at a loss to understand the significance of any of this.'

'But you understand the significance of the Marquis of Sywell, I make no doubt!' she flashed, the brown eyes alight with anger. 'And pray do not tell me that I should not have said anything about him, for that I know already.'

'Then I wonder at your bringing up the name at all! Sywell is scarcely a fit subject for the delicate ears of a female.'

'But fit enough for the indelicacy of males!'

There was a silence. The Viscount eyed her in no small degree of puzzlement, his natural anger dying away. He could make nothing of these remarks. But he was not going to enter into discussion about a man whose name should never have sullied the ears of a girl of eighteen years.

'Are you going to meet Miss Geary? May I escort you?' he asked, in a tone of chilly politeness.

Serena had been listening with horror to the echo in her mind of her own words. How could she have been so unguarded? She had as well have accused Wyndham outright! What had possessed her to mention the Marquis? Yet she was conscious of inordinate disappointment that the Viscount had ignored her comments. It seemed to Serena that this argued a guilty reticence that condemned him.

'No, I thank you,' she said, in an attempt to emulate the coolness of his tone. 'I can very well go by myself.'

Even to her own ears, this sounded more sulky than sophisticated. Forgetting to pick up the two other volumes of her chosen novel, she dropped a curtsey and swept past Wyndham to the counter.

To her dismay—and guilty triumph!—he followed her. But it was only to present her with the other volumes which he had collected on her behalf from the shelf.

'I think you may need these,' he said and, bowing, walked away from her and out of the shop.

He was seething, but determined not to let Serena see it. Her manner had convinced him that her father had spoken less than the truth. She might or might not have transferred her affections to another man, but he could be in no doubt that something had induced her to take himself in aversion. Had she coupled him in some way with the infamous Marquis of Sywell? Impossible! He knew his reputation to be well enough established that no one could accuse him of associating with a reprobate of that cut.

Before he could probe the matter further, he saw Serena come out of Hatchards, holding her package of books. She hesitated for a moment, looking towards the press of carriages down the street. Wyndham was within an ace of renewing his offer of escort when he saw a gentleman detach himself from a knot of men standing together upon the flagway and move to accost Miss Reeth.

He was a florid man, loose-limbed and somewhat careless in his dress, and one whom the Viscount recognised. And not with any degree of pleasure! He knew Hailcombe to be a landless lord, somewhere in his early thirties, who lived by his wits and gaming. He had been lately in His Majesty's naval service, and it was generally rumoured that he had been forced to sell out by the vociferous demands of his seniors.

Wyndham eyed this individual's approach to Serena with considerable disfavour. If this was the fellow whose affections had engaged hers in his stead, he must deem himself most cruelly insulted.

Serena viewed the coming of Hailcombe with no less disfavour. She did not like this bluff friend of her father's, and could have wished that Papa had not invited him to dine with them. He had an abrupt way with him, graceless and unrefined. Serena found him coarse. He had, as he phrased it, 'eaten his mutton' with them on no less than three occasions since they had returned to town. Each time he had devoted more of his attention to the daughter of the house, who had received his clumsy attempts to engage her in conversation with polite indifference.

'Ah, the lovely Miss Reeth!' he hailed her with heavy gallantry. 'Miss Geary awaits you. Allow me to escort you to your carriage. Nothing could afford me greater pleasure.'

It was otherwise with Serena, but she refrained

from saying so. Her attention was so concentrated upon her encounter with the Viscount that this interruption could be nothing but an irritant.

'It is but a step, sir, and I can very well go on my own.'

'What, and expose your prettiness for all the fools of London to gape at?' He doffed his hat and took from her the package of books.

Serena saw no recourse other than to take the arm he thrust upon her, and placed the veriest fingertip upon it, chafing at the dawdling pace.

'I must hurry, sir, for I have already kept my cousin waiting overlong.'

The carriage was standing some twenty-five yards from them, and Serena was relieved to arrive and allow her unwelcome escort to hand her up. But worse was to come.

'Lord Hailcombe, how kind!' said Cousin Laura in what Serena considered to be over-friendly tones. 'Are you walking? Can we take you up? We may easily pass by Half Moon Street on our way, if you should be returning to your lodging.'

To Serena's disgust, Lord Hailcombe accepted with alacrity, and jumped up into the barouche, taking his seat opposite her and ogling her quite dreadfully through his quizzing-glass.

It was really too bad that she should be subjected to such attention from a man nearly twice her age! It was not that his looks were odious, although his cheeks had a tendency to be high-coloured—weatherbeaten, Papa said, from his days at sea. But a pair of full lips and two thick brows gave him an offensively leering look, especially when he smiled.

He did so now, the lips lifting from his teeth in a way that made Serena feel positively nauseous.

'Fortunate I should have chanced upon you, Miss Reeth. Thought of the most delightful scheme. There's a ridotto tomorrow evening. House of a friend of mine. Mrs Henbury—you may have heard of her.'

Serena had not, and she looked instinctively to Cousin Laura, knowing that Papa had strictly enjoined her to permit his daughter to attend only Ton parties. She was astonished, therefore, when her duenna seemed inclined to look upon the invitation with a favourable eye.

'Mrs Henbury? I do not think so. But a ridotto? Such fun for the young folk!'

'My thought exactly. D'you suppose my friend Reeth will allow our young innocent to attend? Under your eye, of course, ma'am.'

Incensed, Serena heard Cousin Laura accepting the invitation, subject only to Papa's agreement. Our young innocent indeed! How dared he speak of her in such terms? As if he had been an uncle, or something of the sort. She was slightly cheered by the reflection that Papa was bound to disapprove, but she could manage only a vague smile when called upon by her duenna to applaud the treat in store.

The house inhabited by Mrs Henbury proved to be situated in an unfashionable quarter of Bloomsbury. Which was just what Serena might have expected of a lady whose name was quite unknown—even to Lissett, who knew everybody!

'No, Miss Serena, I have not heard the name. No doubt one of these hangers-on who live upon the fringes of society.'

There had been no relief afforded by Lord Reeth either. Serena had stood in stunned disbelief as Papa had not only agreed to the arrangement, but had enjoined his daughter to be sure and conduct herself towards Lord Hailcombe with proper deference.

'Let me not be put to the blush by hearing of your having spoken out in that pert manner of which you are sometimes guilty. His lordship is a particular friend of mine, and I desire you will treat him becomingly.'

Feeling betrayed, Serena had barely been able to bring herself to acknowledge this stern admonition. She had murmured what Papa might, if he chose, take for assent, and had dropped a curtsey. Then she had fled to her nursery parlour, there to indulge in a useless rodomontade against Wyndham for proving too unworthy to have rescued her with the betrothal she had so ardently desired.

But here she was, in a large house furnished with the tasteless opulence of gilded sofas in the Egyptian style, and ornate wallpaper of heavy brocade. The only consolation Serena could give herself was that she counted none of the guests among her acquaintance. Which was as well, for the lack of decorum and freedom of manners displayed by many members of the company quite shocked her. Worse was to follow.

Cousin Laura had melted away among the older females, leaving Serena no alternative but to accept Hailcombe's hand for the dance. The room set aside for the purpose was not large, and the press of persons under two massive chandeliers made Serena feel uncomfortably hot.

She had reason to be glad of the forethought that had caused her to choose a modest round gown—of a lemon yellow that suited little with her hair—which offered no real exposure of flesh. For her situation was horrid indeed when she discovered that the figures of the country dance gave her partner unlimited opportunities to touch and squeeze, and slip his arm about her waist. At one instant, Hailcombe contrived even to brush his fingers over the swell of her breast.

Unmindful of her father's warning, she burst out with, 'What are you doing, sir?'

'Doing, ma'am?' said he, wide-eyed with innocence under those heavy eyebrows. 'Why, dancing, m'dear.'

'You touched me!'

'But m'dear Miss Reeth, how am I to avoid it? The figure, ma'am, the figure. What d'you mean?'

'You know very well,' said Serena angrily.

'I don't, but let that pass. Sorry to have offended you. Assure you, it weren't by design. Such a crowd!'

Serena was obliged to accept this. One could not make a scene in public. But she made deliberate efforts to stand away from him for the remainder of the dance, and was at length forced to own that he made no further attempt to do more than take her hand for the requisite movements.

She was relieved, but could not help contrasting Hailcombe's conduct with that of Wyndham. Never, by so much as a look or a touch, had he taken the slightest liberty with her. She had felt so completely safe with him that it had not even occurred to her that he might do so.

It occurred to her forcibly now, however. A libertine, as he had been accused, would be expected to behave in just such a fashion. Or might he do so only with women of a certain class? Gentlemen, so Cousin Laura had instructed her, could keep a mistress among the demi-monde, yet never permit their wives and daughters even to speak of such women. It hurt Serena to think that Wyndham was just such a hypocrite.

To her shame, a sneaking regret came over Serena that Wyndham had not taken any liberties. She could not but admit that if it had been *his* fingers at her waist, she would not have been in the least revolted.

The evening could not have ended too soon, and Serena spent the remainder of it at as much distance from Hailcombe as she could conveniently manage without offence, fanning herself in a manner that hid her face from him for much of the time. She refused every request to dance again, and could not but be glad to see the growing discontent that overlaid the florid features of her escort. She only hoped that he would recognise how unwelcome were his attentions.

* * *

Serena's hope proved misplaced. On Friday, when she attended the play at Drury Lane escorted by Lord Reeth as well as Cousin Laura, she was immediately struck by Lord Hailcombe's appearance in a box opposite which she knew to be occupied by a notorious courtesan. Along with others of her stamp, the woman had been pointed out to her by her conscientious duenna, anxious to prevent her charge from making social gaffes through ignorance.

Serena had refrained from reporting the familiarities that had been taken with her to Cousin Laura. Not from any wish of saving Lord Hailcombe from censure, but because she felt a deep-seated fear that her duenna was capable of condoning even this licentious conduct. But she felt sure that Papa must be disgusted with his friend's public acknowledgement of the female in the box opposite. She knew that Lord Reeth saw it, for she had been within an ace of calling it to his attention when she saw that his eye was fixed upon Hailcombe—and in no very pleasant spirit.

Yet when he entered their box in the next interval, Serena was shocked to see Papa greet him with great affability. Indeed, the Baron went so far as to give up his seat, saying that no doubt Hailcombe wished to converse with his daughter.

Serena had barely got over this, and was with some difficulty parrying the ogling remarks addressed to her, when she saw that Viscount Wyndham was standing in the pit, his gaze trained upon their box. Since its situation was on the lowest level, he was at no great distance from them, and could not avoid re-cognising her company.

It was with mixed feelings that Serena noted the disapproval in his face. She was ashamed to be dis-covered by him with Hailcombe in attendance. Yet she could not but be angry at his daring to look cen-soriously, when by all accounts his own conduct left a great deal to be desired. Matters were not helped when Hailcombe chose to refer to it.

'See, Miss Reeth, what jealousy you inspire?'

Serena turned to look at him, feeling her colour mounting. 'I do not take your meaning, sir.'

Hailcombe tittered, his thick lips curling in some-thing perilously close to a sneer. 'Why, I speak of your rejected suitor there. Almost sorry for the poor fellow, though I'm the richer for his discomfiture.'

A flame of anger lit Serena's breast. 'How did you know that Wyndham had been rejected?'

'Inference, Miss Reeth,' he responded, smiling with disgusting superiority. 'Just inference.' He leaned to-wards her in a pose distressingly intimate, lowering his voice to a murmur. 'Glad your tastes run on dif-ferent lines. You're a sensible girl. You can see the advantage of maturity.'

Serena was struck dumb. She could not mistake the tenor of this speech. She knew not what to reply, for the thought of what must be in his mind made her sick to her stomach. She cast a wild glance around, as if in search of rescue, and her frantic eyes met those of Lord Wyndham.

He had shifted his position, and was standing

within a few feet of her. Without thought, Serena threw up her fan, plying it so that it hid her face momentarily from Hailcombe's sight.

Under cover of this temporary veil, she mouthed a desperate plea to Wyndham. 'Pray help me!'

Whether he caught it she could not tell, for at that instant the action began again upon the stage. Thankfully, Lord Reeth resumed his seat as Hailcombe vacated it and left the box. By the time Serena had leisure to look around once more for the Viscount, he was no longer there.

Saturday dawned grey and overcast, the drizzle at the window all too much in keeping with Serena's mood. She did not know whether she was more upset with Hailcombe for his untimely hints, or with Wyndham for ignoring her impulsive appeal.

Ringing for her maid, she requested her breakfast on a tray. 'I am feeling too weary to rise this early, Mary. I shall stay in bed and read my novel.'

'Oh, but his lordship asked me special if you was up, Miss Serena,' said Mary, 'for he wishes to speak to you as soon as ever you was ready to go downstairs.'

These were most unwelcome tidings. What in the world could Papa want with her? Had he seen that look she had cast at the Viscount? Perhaps he'd had word from someone that she had been seen talking to him in Hatchards. Not that Papa could expect that she might avoid Wyndham altogether since he was bound to be at the same gatherings as she attended. But if he supposed her disobedient to his wishes, Papa could be unpleasantly severe.

All desire to take breakfast had disappeared. Instead, Serena bade Mary help her to dress. It felt as if it took an age to array herself in a white muslin gown, long-sleeved, with an overgown patterned in a simple sprig that added much needed warmth. Throughout, Serena's mind ran upon horrid visions of Papa's displeasure, and the probable reasons for it. By the time she was dressed, she had convinced herself that a scold awaited her, and anxiety had rendered her nauseous.

But when at last she entered the library, her father rose from behind his desk and greeted her in a perfectly affable way. Indeed, he was almost too full of bonhomie for his daughter's comfort.

'Serena, my dear child, very good of you to come to me so quickly. Have you eaten? No? Now what was Mary about to hurry you so? After breakfast would have done as well.'

'I—I was anxious to know what you could want with me, Papa,' Serena ventured.

Reeth laughed in a way that sounded false to Serena's ears. 'My dear girl, you are surely not in fear of your papa? You know I have always your interests at heart.'

Serena knew not how to reply to this. It had not been Papa's practice to seek her out merely for the pleasure of her company! It was not as if he doted upon her. If anyone was the object of Lord Reeth's caressing affection, it was her only surviving sibling.

Little Gerald, whose birth had been the occasion of their Mama's sad demise, was but five years of age and heir to the family estates in Suffolk, whither his fond father betook himself whenever he could spare time from his activities in government. Perhaps he was cosseted because his were the shoulders upon which the Reeth inheritance rested. But Serena knew that her own doting fondness for her brother did not exceed that of their papa.

'Sit down, Serena,' her father adjured her, flinging himself into one of the huge leather chairs placed either side of the fireplace.

Unaccountably nervous again, Serena sat down on the edge of the chair opposite, looking at her parent with a good deal of misgiving. She could not help but realise that Papa was most uncharacteristically ill-at-ease. He kept uncrossing and recrossing his legs, all the while with his eyes trained first upon the fire, and then upon the large timepiece that adorned the mantel. At length, he cleared his throat and turned his gaze upon his daughter. Serena held her breath.

'I have asked you here, my child, because I have made up my mind upon the subject of your future.'

A flutter disturbed the breath in Serena's bosom. Even had she thought of anything to say, she could not have opened her mouth to answer him.

'It was remiss of me not to have made some such arrangement at the outset,' Lord Reeth went on. 'Had your mama been alive, of course, none of this would have fallen upon my shoulders. And Laura, I am obliged to admit, has turned out to be unfitted to be a judge of these matters.'

Some inkling of where Papa was headed began to penetrate Serena's brain. It had all to do with Wyndham's turning out to have been unworthy. Was it Papa's intention to make her choice for her? A hideous premonition seized her.

'You have arranged a marriage for me!' she blurted out.

'No, not that,' said her father quickly. 'Not quite that. I hope I am not so Gothic in this day and age as to order you to give yourself to the man whom I would prefer you to choose.'

The Roman nose was thrust into the air, and that severity of countenance that Serena dreaded overlaid Papa's features.

'However,' he said heavily, 'I must say that I will be disappointed, Serena—most disappointed indeed!—if you should choose to thwart my wishes in this matter.'

Serena swallowed uncomfortably. Her voice felt thick and unwieldy in her throat. 'Who—may I ask who…?'

She faded out, unable to finish the question for the dread that rose up to choke her. An unwelcome image popped into her head. Papa could not have *him* in mind! Even the name in her head made her ill to think of it.

Lord Reeth cleared his throat again, and Serena saw, with a vague sense of disquiet under the dread, that he shifted once more in that fidgety way that was so unlike him.

'I have thought long and hard on the subject, my child, and I have decided that it will be safest for you to ally yourself with a man of mature years. One whom, I have reason to believe, is in a fair way to doting upon you. He has asked my permission to address you, and I have assured him of my support.'

Serena's tongue gave way. 'You cannot mean Lord Hailcombe! Oh, Papa, pray say it is not he!'

To her alarm, her father's cheeks became suffused with colour. 'Good God, girl, will you defy me so readily? I hope you are not going to tell me that you have taken Hailcombe in dislike. Have I not already given you to understand that he is a particular friend of mine? That alone should have secured your sympathy!'

She was on her feet. 'Pray, Papa, don't be angry with me! I am sorry for it, but I confess I cannot like him. As for marrying him—I could not!'

Reeth arose also, turning away to march across to his desk, in a hasty manner that told his daughter how much she had displeased him. He spoke without turning round.

'You must learn to like him, Serena. It is not only my wish, but my command.'

'But, Papa,' she uttered desperately, following him a little way and addressing herself to his unresponsive back, 'you said you would not force me! You said you were not so Gothic as to—'

Reeth swung round upon her, eyes blazing. 'Do

you dare to throw my words back in my face? Don't
try me too far, Serena! I am well aware of the reason
for your recalcitrance. You had not been averse to
Hailcombe had it not been for this foolish fancy you
have developed for Wyndham.'

Serena's voice trembled. 'Indeed, Papa, it is n-not
so! Pray, pray b-believe that I would have disliked
Lord Hailcombe even had I not f-formed a p-partiality
for Lord Wyndham.'

'Poppycock! Do you think me a fool?'

'No, Papa, but—'

'Don't talk to me!' flared her father, striding away
again to lash about the room, almost as if he could
not bear to look at her. 'My own daughter to defy me
to my face! How can you say you dislike him? You
barely know him! And to refuse to accede to my request. Cannot you see that you will put me in an
extremely awkward position? I have given my word
to Hailcombe—' He broke off, stopping short and
glaring at Serena. 'However, that is neither here nor
there. But don't imagine that I will relent towards
Wyndham, for I won't!'

Serena was shaking in her shoes, but she was quite
as determined as her father. And she was fighting for
her whole future! She must try what she might to
placate him.

'I do not think of Lord Wyndham, Papa. Cousin
Laura told me something of—of the Marquis of
Sywell, and I quite see that he is not a fit person
for me.'

'In that case, you should have no difficulty in turning your thoughts upon another.'

'Yes, if it were any other than Lord Hailcombe!' she burst out before she could stop herself.

Too late, she saw that her words had enraged Papa still further. Marching to the door, he dragged it open.

'Out of my sight! Until you can assure me of your obedience, I have no wish to see or speak to you again.'

Chapter Three

Stunned by this harsh ultimatum, Serena stared at Papa's unrelenting features. But there was no softening in them as they glared back at her. A vivid memory of Wyndham's face came into her mind—as hatefully cold. Her heart swept with a sensation of loneliness, Serena dropped her eyes and walked swiftly past her father, and out of the room.

She heard the door slam behind her, and flew upstairs to her nursery parlour, there to jerk up and down the little room, her thoughts all chaos. Dashing unregarded tears from her cheeks, she found herself raging as savagely as had Papa.

How could he treat her so? What possessed him to take this sudden decision? And to declare it to be unalterable! Never had he shown himself so unmindful of her preferences.

And to become obsessed with Hailcombe of all people! Why, he was not even eligible. The title into which he had told them he had recently come was neither an old nor a worthy one. His predecessor, he had said, had so wasted his inheritance as to lose the lands that had gone with the barony. He had even boasted of his luck at cards, which enabled him to support himself as a gentleman.

Why, he was a man whom Lord Reeth might have been depended upon to despise! Wyndham was worth a dozen of him. But Papa had taken against the Viscount, even without real proof of his guilt. Serena had not doubted Papa's wisdom in blighting her hopes. But in the face of his championing of Hailcombe, she dared to wonder.

Before she could pursue this thought, the door opened to admit Cousin Laura, who rustled into the room in her grey silk gown. Serena stiffened, fearing a lecture on her falling out with Papa. But it seemed that her duenna had not yet been made mistress of the occurrence.

'My dear Serena, what do you think?' she said excitedly, waving a letter. 'We have been invited to a house party at Lacey Court. It is to be for a week, and we are requested to go next Friday.'

Serena had never heard of Lacey Court, but the thought of removing from London at this time was only too welcome.

'Who lives at Lacey Court, cousin?'

'Why, it is the home of Sir Lucius Lacey. No, you are not acquainted with him, for I believe he rarely comes to London. You may have met his wife and his daughter, who came out last season. But I believe, dear child, that it must have been Lady Camelford who arranged it, for I have had the kindest note from her informing me that she is to be of the party, together with her son.' She frowned, removing her spectacles. 'I must say I cannot understand what motivates her. Her son has just become betrothed, so it cannot be that she thinks of him for you.'

Serena refrained from informing her that it would be in vain if Lady Camelford had any such notion, even had her son not been engaged. There was time enough for Cousin Laura to find out what her father had planned for her destiny.

But the lure of freedom gave Serena furiously to think. It was of the first importance to discover whether Lord Hailcombe was also to be at Lacey Court. Unlikely, for his acquaintance did not appear to be with people of the first consequence. Which made Papa's partiality the more incomprehensible. If Hailcombe was not to be present, it was probable that Papa would refuse his consent to the scheme. Particularly if he believed her to be still rebellious.

By Sunday morning, it was abundantly plain not only that Cousin Laura had been primed, but that her father was adamant. Breakfast on the Lord's day was always taken by the family together, prior to attending morning service at St George's in the square. This habit was adhered to, but Lord Reeth neither looked at his daughter throughout, nor addressed her by a single word. Cousin Laura, casting nervous glances at him from time to time, applied herself to her meal in between uttering a stream of inane remarks to Serena, accompanied by such facial contortions of warning as almost caused her charge to giggle—despite the severe discomfort brought about by Papa's attitude.

When Lord Reeth swept out of the room, with a general admonition to the ladies to hurry, the duenna seized the opportunity to whisper a frantic admonition.

'Do not anger him further, my child! We shall talk of it when we return from church, and I do hope I may persuade you to see reason.'

Which made Serena look forward to the coming discussion with strong misgiving. Cousin Laura had clearly been suborned by Papa into furthering his aim. Not that she had a choice. Her duenna was dependent upon Papa's good will. She had served him well in the capacity of surrogate mother to his children, but Serena knew her father was capable of parting company with Cousin Laura if she went against him. And then the only future she could hope for was to take up a post as companion or governess, just as she had done before being called upon by Papa when Mama had expired.

But merely because Cousin Laura had to support Papa was no reason why Serena should succumb to his tyrannical decree! A sentiment which she did not scruple to express when the promised tête-à-tête took place in the nursery parlour.

'But, my dear child,' protested Cousin Laura, 'you cannot wish to be at outs with your papa. Besides, it is most unfair to accuse him of tyranny.'

'What then do you call it?' demanded Serena rebelliously. 'Well, I am more his daughter than he knows! He will soon learn that I can be just as stubborn.'

Her duenna groaned. 'Serena, pray don't! It is so uncomfortable for us all. Won't you at least try to like Lord Hailcombe?'

At this, Serena was moved to condemn both his lordship's manners and morals, and to give her duenna a word picture of the liberties he had taken with her at Mrs Henbury's.

'Serena, why did you not tell me?' clucked Cousin Laura, shocked. 'Perhaps I should tell your papa of this.'

'It will make no difference,' Serena told her, dropping abruptly into despondency. 'Papa does not even like Hailcombe, I am persuaded. What drives him to this I do not know, but he is certainly determined upon this marriage.'

It occurred to her all at once that her duenna must have known of this several days ago.

'Papa told you to encourage Hailcombe, didn't he, Cousin Laura?' she accused. 'Else you could not have thought of inviting him into the carriage that day in Piccadilly. Nor would you have taken me to such a dreadful house as that Mrs Henbury inhabited!'

Looking extremely guilty, Miss Geary removed her spectacles and fiddled with them in her lap. 'Your papa told me he believes Lord Hailcombe to be a man of sense,' she said evasively. 'It is not his fault, your papa says, that his inheritance has been wasted, and Bernard thinks that a man who has known hardship may be depended on to develop a habit of providence.

He is truly thinking of your happiness, my dear child, for he has chosen for you a gentleman whose suitability does not depend upon worldly considerations.'

Serena's response was sceptical. 'If he was thinking of my happiness, cousin, he would not force me into marriage against my will.'

'But he is not forcing you to it, child. He has merely requested—'

'He has *commanded*, cousin, not requested. And he delivered an ultimatum that has hurt me very much.'

Cousin Laura tutted in a despairing way, shuffling her spectacles on and off her nose several times. Presently, she looked again to the chair by the fireplace where Serena was sitting.

'Do you know, Serena, I believe your poor papa was himself much hurt by your refusal to listen to his proposal. You are so impetuous, my dear. If only you would let him see that you are willing to be dutiful and obedient, perhaps he will listen to you with more patience.'

'But I am not willing,' Serena protested. 'Why should I pretend that I will consider Hailcombe when nothing in the world would induce me to accept him?'

Cousin Laura replaced her spectacles and through them gave her charge a straight look. 'I am much afraid that if you do not make your peace with your papa, my child, you will not be permitted to go to Lacey Court.'

Serena studied her duenna's eyes through the round panes. Was Cousin Laura beginning to come around to her side? Had she too realised that such a remove must offer a respite from this intolerable demand of Papa's?

Cousin Laura said no more, but excused herself and went away. More than ever, Serena determined to find out whether Hailcombe was to be at Lacey Court.

Her opportunity came upon the following day, when he arrived in Hanover Square to invite her for a drive in the park. Twenty-four hours earlier, Serena would have unhesitatingly refused. But with Cousin Laura's words in her mind, she decided to kill two birds with one stone.

'Thank you, sir, I will be very happy. Only give me a moment to put on my hat and pelisse.'

Wholly ignoring the astonishment in Cousin Laura's face, she ran upstairs to her bedchamber. Five minutes later, she was in the hall, clad in a charming bonnet with a dashing plume that admirably matched the green pelisse. Her escort bowed her out of the house, but in the doorway she halted.

'Oh, Lissett, pray inform my father that I am gone to the park with Lord Hailcombe,' she said airily to the butler.

'As you wish, Miss Serena.'

She was handed up into the curricle, which was drawn, most unfashionably, only by a pair of horses. Hailcombe, attired in a great-coat of yellow drab, took up the reins; his groom let go the greys' heads and leapt up nimbly behind.

During the drive, Serena adopted a cool manner towards Hailcombe, designed to give him no more encouragement than was contained in her apparent willingness to accompany him. She kept a rigid control over her tongue, and answered his every attempt to engage in dalliance with obvious detachment.

When they turned into the gates of Hyde Park, to Serena's dismay Hailcombe dispensed with the services of his groom. Aside from having no wish to be seen alone with him in a carriage, it opened the way for a tête-à-tête which was not at all to her taste. His first words confirmed this.

'By my faith, Miss Reeth, I believe your attention is otherwhere,' he accused in a petulant tone.

Serena turned a limpid gaze upon him. 'No, indeed, sir. I would not be so impolite as to allow my attention to be distracted from my escort.'

Hailcombe was silent for a moment or two, evidently ruminating. Serena perforce bowed to an acquaintance in a passing barouche, feeling relieved that the cold must prevent many members of the Ton from taking the air.

When Hailcombe addressed her again, it was a trifle offhandedly. 'Wonder if your father has spoken to you.'

'Not recently.' Aware of the give-away flatness in her tone, she added quickly, 'I do not see a deal of Papa. He is seldom at home, and only occasionally accompanies us to parties.'

A hard note entered Hailcombe's voice. 'I meant, ma'am, has he spoken to you of me?'

Serena turned to look at him, widening her eyes. 'Why, yes, sir. He speaks of you with affection.'

'No, I don't mean—'

He broke off, pouting his heavy lips in a look of ill-humour. Serena hoped that she had led him to imagine that his way had not yet been smoothed. She waved to a young lady she knew in as nonchalant a fashion as she could manage, and decided she had best embark upon the subject that had brought her out on this excursion.

'I must tell you that I have received a most flattering invitation, my lord.'

'Yes?' It was grunted out, Hailcombe appearing abstracted.

'To a house party at Lacey Court. Do you know it?'

'Don't believe I do.'

'It is the home of Sir Lucius Lacey, and I think it was Lady Camelford who recommended me to his notice.'

There was discontent in Hailcombe's voice. 'Do you make a long stay there?'

'I hardly know,' Serena fibbed. 'A week or two, I dare say.'

'Reeth gives his permission, does he?'

A note of vague menace seemed to underlie this question. Serena felt impelled to prevaricate, for she was suddenly sure that Hailcombe would question her father on the matter.

'Papa would not wish me to offend Lady Camelford. She is the wife of one of his closest associates, you must know.'

'But he has no obligation to Sir Lucius Lacey.'

Serena was silent, conscious of a stirring of unease.

Hailcombe had lost his tone of bluff flirtation. His heavy brows were drawn together, and there was a harshness in his words that made her glad she had held out against Papa. Once again she felt that sense of question about her father's motives in supporting this man's application for her hand.

'You don't know of Lord Wyndham's relationship to Sir Lucius Lacey then?' asked Hailcombe, a sneer in his voice.

At the mention of his lordship's name, a flutter leapt into life in Serena's chest, and she was cast into immediate confusion.

'I d-didn't know,' she stuttered helplessly. 'What is—what relation is he?'

'Wyndham's uncle, as I'll warrant your father knows all too well.'

The implication was clear, as was the depth into which Hailcombe was in Lord Reeth's confidence. He already knew of the Viscount's rejection, and now it seemed he also knew the reason for it. A flame of anger leapt in her breast. It was not for Hailcombe to judge Wyndham's character! How dared he take it upon himself to warn her, even obliquely, that Papa was bound to refuse his consent? No doubt he would take care to inform Papa of the fatal relationship, should he not already be aware of it.

Despair lent her inspiration. 'If that is the case, I hardly think his lordship will be present. He cannot wish to endure the embarrassment of being at close quarters with a lady who has determined against him.'

Hailcombe gave her a straight look. 'But have you determined against him?'

'Since you are clearly master of what passed between my father and his lordship, sir,' Serena pointed out, betrayed into forgetting to guard her speech, 'I imagine you must know very well that I am so determined. I do not know why my father should choose to confide in you, my lord, but he plainly does, and I therefore do not scruple to mention the circumstances which have induced me to take against Lord Wyndham.'

'Such ugly circumstances, don't you think?'

Serena was obliged to bite down upon a heated retort. 'I am happy to say that I know nothing of the details.'

'But enough to turn you away from his lordship, eh?'

It was on the tip of her tongue to refute this. To her shame, she realised that even the worst of the excesses that had been related to her by Cousin Laura had failed to turn her thoughts from the Viscount. But it would not do to say so.

'I have put him quite out of my mind.'

A smile drew the full lips apart, but it was not pleasant. 'Like to believe you, m'dear, but it's a poor liar you are.'

It was too much. Serena lost her temper. 'I don't care whether you believe me or not, Lord Hailcombe. But this you may believe. However strong my dislike of Wyndham's way of life, it could not possibly be as deep as my dislike of you!'

There was a breathless pause. Time enough for Serena to regret her hasty words, and experience a flare of apprehension for the consequences.

'If that's the case,' Hailcombe growled at last, 'I'd best lose no time in returning you home.'

Serena made no answer, and the drive back to Hanover Square was accomplished in silence.

Entering the house in a mood of severe apprehension, Serena was guiltily aware of having spiked her own guns. She could not doubt that Hailcombe would speak to Papa. Even if her rudeness induced the man to draw off—which she dared not suppose to be likely—Papa was bound to forbid her to go to Lacey Court.

She had already set her foot on the stair when she became aware that Lissett, who had let her in, was hovering in a manner that indicated a wish for speech with her.

'You want me, Lissett?'

The butler bowed. 'His lordship requested that you should go directly to the saloon upon your return, Miss Serena.'

These ominous words struck Serena with instant dread. She gazed upon Lissett's kindly features, her heart jumping. 'He wishes to s-see me?'

'He does, Miss Serena. I gave him your message, like you asked.' A reassuring smile was bent upon her. 'His lordship seemed pleased.'

To what avail, when her subsequent conduct must inevitably infuriate him? Remembering, however, that he could not yet know of it, Serena took heart. Thanking the butler, she ran up the stairs and went directly to the saloon, forgetting in her haste that she was still clad for the outdoors.

The elegant first-floor saloon was done out in the discretion of straw and cream that gave it both light and a sensation of spaciousness. Entering in haste, Serena stopped short, startled to discover that Papa was not alone.

Lord Reeth was in a chair to one side of the fireplace, opposite a sofa upon which were seated Cousin Laura and a female of matronly aspect, fashionably dressed in imposing purple with a yellow turban all over feathers.

'Lady Camelford! I—I thought—'

'Good gracious, Serena!' broke in Cousin Laura, shocked. 'Why could you not have put off your pelisse and hat? Lady Camelford will think you a sad romp!'

'Nothing of the sort,' contradicted the lady, smiling graciously.

'I b-beg your p-pardon, ma'am,' stammered Serena, unbuttoning the offending garment. 'You see, I was told that Papa wished to see me at once, and I—'

'And you naturally hurried to obey the summons. I quite understand. But perhaps you should ring for your maid?'

'Thank you, yes.' Crossing hastily to the fireplace, and avoiding her father's eye, Serena tugged at the bell-pull. Turning back to the visitor, she recalled an omission, and dropped a curtsey. 'How do you do, ma'am?'

The matron looked amused. 'I am well, I thank you, Serena.' She held out a hand, and Serena put hers into it, feeling a warm clasp close over her fingers. Her ladyship spoke confidingly. 'I have been persuading your Papa to allow you to make one of the party at Lacey Court.'

Serena's eyes flew to her father's face. There was a relaxation in his features of the sternness to which she had hitherto been subjected. Reeth did not quite smile, but he nodded to his daughter.

'You are to go,' he said succinctly, rising. 'And now, if you will excuse me, ma'am, I have work to do.'

'Yes, yes, run along,' urged Lady Camelford, releasing Serena's hand. 'I am used to being abandoned for the demands of politics!'

To Serena's relief, Papa laughed out at this sally, and bowing briefly, withdrew. She slipped off her pelisse and threw it carelessly onto a chair, revealing beneath it a plain little gown of white spotted muslin.

Cousin Laura rose to help her off with the bonnet. 'Is it not kind of your dear papa, Serena? And so extremely generous of you, Lady Camelford, to take an interest in the child.'

'Yes, and I must thank you, ma'am,' agreed Serena, moving to take her father's vacated chair. She added involuntarily, 'Though I wonder that you should take me up in this fashion.'

'Serena!' hissed her duenna, who was busy tidying the discarded attire.

But Lady Camelford was laughing. 'I could prevaricate and say that I wish only to please your father, but the truth is that I had great difficulty in prevailing upon him to agree to the scheme. He was most unwilling to let you out of his sight, was he not, Miss Geary? I had no notion of his being so doting a father!'

Neither had Serena, but she refrained from saying so. She could only marvel at the good luck that had brought Lady Camelford upon this errand before Papa could have any inkling of her disgraceful rudeness to Hailcombe.

'It is fortunate,' said Cousin Laura, with a meaning look at Serena as she retook her seat, 'that his lordship was particularly pleased with his daughter's conduct just at the moment. He was brought to agree, my child, that you deserved this treat.'

Was this meant to convey that Papa had been induced to believe her to have had a change of heart because she had driven out with Hailcombe? How speedily he was going to be undeceived! Serena hardly dared hope that he would honour his decision to let her go to Lacey Court.

A knock at the door at this moment produced the butler, come in answer to the summons of the bell, and Cousin Laura requested him to send in Mary to her mistress.

The interlude served to deepen Serena's puzzlement. Upon Lissett's leaving the saloon, she did not hesitate to voice it.

'If Papa was so difficult to persuade, I understand even less, ma'am, why you should go to so much trouble on my behalf.'

She saw Cousin Laura's frown of admonishment, but Lady Camelford forestalled any comment. A peculiarly conscious look crossed her strong features.

'If you will have it, my dear, I hope you will not be offended. Truthfully, I am acting not on your behalf, but on that of my prospective daughter-in-law.'

A recollection threw Serena into speech. 'Oh, your son is to marry Miss Lacey! It had not until this moment struck me that she must be related to Sir Lucius.'

Cousin Laura started. 'Good gracious, yes! She is his daughter.'

And therefore Wyndham's cousin! But this Serena kept to herself. A pattering started up in her pulses. Could it be that this invitation had been issued at the Viscount's intervention?

'But I do not—I do know Miss Lacey,' she faltered. 'At least, I have met her, only—'

'I see I shall have to confess it all,' sighed Lady Camelford, her eyes dancing in the mock solemnity of her face. 'Melanie is the liveliest creature. I am already almost as fond of her as is my dear John. You see, the Little Season has brought few of her own friends to town. The dear child came herself only for a short visit, just to see me. And she begged me to think of one or two young persons who might be induced to join the party, for according to Mel, it is to be composed of "the most dreadful collection of old fogies"!' Here Lady Camelford burst into laughter. 'Really, she is a shocking child! But one cannot help loving her.'

'And so you thought of Serena,' put in Cousin Laura.

'My mind naturally roved among the children of my political acquaintance,' agreed Lady Camelford. 'But it was Mel who selected you, my dear Serena. She had an impression, she said, that you would add spice to the occasion.'

Both the visitor and Cousin Laura looked as if they could not imagine why. Nor indeed, could the subject of this peculiar choice. But Serena was less concerned with this aspect of the matter, than with the clear implication that she had been chosen at random. Wyndham could have had nothing to do with it.

Lacey Court was a sprawling mansion, of no definite date. It looked as if its various inhabitants had impulsively added to its bulk with abandon, and no thought of fitting in with the architecture of the place. Which, as Miss Lacey informed Serena, had been precisely the case.

'The whole place is higgledy-piggledy,' said Melanie gaily. 'You may believe for a moment that you are in the Tudor wing, and instantly find yourself transported to Italy in the very next room! And the follies that have been committed upon the gardens have to be seen to be believed. I am sure Capability Brown must have been off his head!'

Serena was obliged to laugh, as she followed her young hostess through the bewildering corridors to find the chamber to which she had been assigned. She had taken an instant liking to the lively Melanie Lacey, and found it easy to understand why Lady Camelford had succumbed.

Miss Lacey had greeted her with a shriek of delight, and enfolded her in a stifling embrace. For Melanie was built on queenly lines, with a merry face and a quantity of chestnut hair which she wore piled in a topknot with ringlets falling down the back. She was engagingly breezy, and embarrassingly forth-right.

'I have so wanted to meet you, Miss Reeth! Oh, no—how stupidly formal. You won't mind if I call you Serena? And you are so beautiful! How I shall scold George for letting you slip through his fingers, the silly fellow!'

Dazed by this eloquence, Serena had been able only to gaze at her, stuttering a confused greeting. 'Th-thank you, Miss Lacey. It is k-kind of you to—to—'

'Oh, stuff! Pray don't say that, for I am so grateful for your presence, I cannot tell you. I wish you will call me Mel. Everyone does. And we are going to be great friends, on that I am determined.'

'Are—are we?' had asked Serena doubtfully.

Melanie had burst out laughing. 'Don't look so dis-mayed! Of course we are.' She had tucked a confiding hand into Serena's arm and begun to lead her to the stairs, Cousin Laura trailing in their wake. 'I have heard so much about you, that I almost feel as if I know you already.'

Serena had been at a loss to know how her hostess could have heard anything about her, and had said so.

'But from George, of course,' Melanie had told her, looking amazed. 'He said that you were very shy— which I see is indeed the case—and also that you had a tendency to blurt out anything that was in your head. "Like me," I said. But George would have it that whereas I had cultivated a habit of saying just what I liked without caring what anyone thought of me—which I must tell you is perfectly true!—you, on the other hand, were apt to be regretful about having said it. Which, George says, is one of the most endearing things about you. As you may suppose, I immediately took him to task for not making up his mind months ago, while he still had an opportunity to attach you. For my part, I should think he must have windmills in his head, for anyone can see that you would have made him the perfect wife!'

By this time it had been borne in upon Serena that Melanie's 'George' was none other than her cousin, George Lyford, Viscount Wyndham. The freedom with which she had spoken of his suit had not unnaturally struck Serena to tense silence, and she had heard Cousin Laura faintly clucking behind her. Fortunately their hostess, whose tongue ran like a fiddlestick, had already moved on to discourse upon the ramifications of Lacey Court, and had been too much involved in her own diatribe to notice.

Serena found herself installed in a sunny bedchamber on the first floor, which gave onto some gardens to one side of the wing. The architect of Serena's new surroundings was obviously a follower of Adam, for a decorative pattern of vine-leaves ran over the mantel and created panels in the pastel shaded walls. The Sheraton furnishings were all of light woods with curving slim legs, and the four-poster was crowned with a circular tester from which billowed curtains of pink silk.

Her duenna was housed in an adjacent room of similar proportions, but with furnishings of so different a style that Serena could not but recognise the truth of Melanie's strictures. Dark wood panelling and hangings of red velvet gave a plush feel of luxury to the chamber, as well as a sense of having crossed into a different historical era. Cousin Laura looked upon it with distaste, but was moved—no doubt by the indiscreet chattering of Melanie Lacey!—to remind her charge of the injunction laid upon her by her father.

'I am not like to forget, cousin,' said Serena flatly, for the horrors of the last three days were not soon to be wiped from her memory.

The Baron, having received an account of the fateful carriage ride from Hailcombe, had stalked into his daughter's nursery parlour in order to deliver a tirade which had at first blasted all hope of Serena's attending the house party. Among a number of other threats, Serena had found herself in imminent danger of being

sent home to Suffolk in disgrace. Papa had not scrupled to warn her that she need not think herself too
much the young lady to receive a well-deserved chas-
tisement with the rod, and had promised that this
should be her fate if Hailcombe had any further cause
to complain of her impertinence.

Having reduced his daughter to mute dread, his
lordship had summarily forbidden the visit to Lacey
Court, and slammed out of the room. Cousin Laura,
an appalled spectator of this ugly scene, had amazed
Serena by embracing her and roundly condemning her
cousin, Hailcombe himself and men in general.

'It is the unfairness of it all that makes me so angry,' she had declared. 'One has so little choice as it
is when one is a female. But when these wretched
men must needs resort to bullying tactics—and upon
those who are necessarily weaker than themselves—
it is really too bad!'

This had been surprising enough. But it had been
entirely owing to Cousin Laura that Papa, in the end,
had been induced to withdraw his objections. Waiting
until his temper should have had time to cool, the
duenna had bravely bearded the lion in his den, and
come away triumphant.

'I was most unscrupulous,' she had told her charge
guiltily, 'for I am afraid I stooped to pretence. Now
if you will only do your part, my child, we may all
come about.'

Papa had been persuaded that a week away would
afford his daughter a period of quiet reflection, in
which Cousin Laura had undertaken to bring her to a

proper frame of mind—although she had no real expectation of Serena's paying the slightest attention to her. She had dared to suggest that Reeth's present methods had only awakened Serena's rebellious spirit, and had put it to him that a softer approach might produce the result he wanted. She had also pointed out that Lady Camelford might be seriously offended if Serena cried off.

Serena had been enjoined to feign gratitude for Papa's relenting, and to submit herself to the indignity of writing an apology to Hailcombe. She had hated the necessity, but she had done it. The result had been all that she dreaded. Her suitor had invited her and Cousin Laura to the theatre, where his assiduous attentions in public must, Serena felt certain, have advertised to the world at large the notion that she was preparing to receive his addresses.

Dreading the all too real possibility that she was going to be coerced into this hateful marriage, Serena had left for Middlesex with unalloyed relief. At least she had this one week of freedom. But any secret hope she might have cherished had been put to flight by Papa's final injunction.

'Should Wyndham happen to be present, Serena, you will oblige me by keeping a proper distance. Do you understand?'

The menace underlying that last had brought his earlier threat of violence forcibly to mind. Inwardly shuddering, she had consented, her tone subdued enough that her father had expressed himself satisfied of her being obedient.

It came therefore as a hideous shock to find herself seated at dinner that first night between an elderly cleric on the one side, and on the other, Viscount Wyndham.

Chapter Four

The immediate symptoms that beset Serena were dismayingly contrary to the behest of Papa. Her heart hammered in her chest, and she felt a touch faint. She could only be glad that she was already sitting down before she became aware of Wyndham's presence beside her. His attention was engaged by the lady on his other side, but it could not be long before he turned to Serena.

Gripping her fingers together in her lap, she strove for calm, glancing across to where her duenna was gazing narrowly at her. She caught Cousin Laura's eye, and a minatory frown was directed upon her. Serena gave a slight nod to show that she had understood. Although how she could 'keep a proper distance' in these circumstances, she was at a loss to imagine.

A plate appeared in front of her, containing a shell full of buttered crab, and several thin strips of toast. Serena stared at it as if she knew not what she must do with it.

'Do you dislike crab, Miss Reeth?'

Serena jumped, turning her head. The sight of the Viscount's warm smile quite melted her bones. Her tongue seemed to have deserted her. She had no idea how her eyes mirrored the disorder of her mind.

Wyndham had envisioned this moment in a spirit compound of mischief and pleasurable anticipation. He had known that Serena must be startled, and had half expected to be roundly taken to task—for he could not doubt that she would speedily fathom his hand in the unexpected invitation.

What he had not bargained for was the abrupt jolt at his chest occasioned by the disconcerted look in the lovely eyes. He was seized with a desire to catch her up and hold her in a comforting embrace—which was impossible. Instead he raised his brows in a teasing look, reached out for the appropriate fork, and gently placed it in her fingers.

Serena blushed and looked away from him, stabbing at the crab shell in a manner that threatened to jerk its contents in all directions. Wyndham sought his mind for a topic which might steady her.

'How did you enjoy *Sense and Sensibility*?' he asked in a carefully neutral tone.

'What? I mean—yes, thank you,' came the low-voiced answer. She appeared to realise that her response was inadequate. Throwing the briefest of glances in his direction, she faltered, 'No—that's not right. What should I say?'

'The novel you selected from Hatchards?' he prompted.

'Oh, yes. How silly! But I have not yet read it. At least, I began it, but…'

She faded out again, daunted by the impossibility of explaining the circumstances that had intervened to prevent her from finishing the book. Her pulse was calming a little, however, and she made an effort to begin upon her repast, digging with the utmost care into the crab shell and bringing forth a dainty portion.

Wyndham watched the quivering fingers lift the fork towards her mouth. It was poised there a moment, and then returned abruptly to the plate.

'I can't eat this!'

'Then don't,' he advised. 'I must say that I am not myself partial to shellfish.'

'It is not that,' Serena uttered, and immediately regretted it. In a rush of conscience, she turned to him, her voice an urgent whisper. 'It is intolerable to be so placed, my lord! Did you arrange it?'

He did not answer for a moment, but the grey eyes regarded her in a considering way. When he spoke, he did not respond directly to her question.

'Do you recall our last meeting—at Drury Lane? Perhaps I should not call it a meeting precisely, for we did not speak.'

Serena eyed him in some puzzlement. 'What are you at?'

A gleam entered his eyes. 'Why, Miss Reeth, can you have forgotten? How could I resist so poignant an appeal?'

All at once Serena remembered it. That look she

had cast him from behind her fan! She felt her cheeks grow warm, and looked quickly away.

'I had forgotten. So much has happened that—' The dreadful circumstances of her present situation came in on her, and she looked at him again. 'There is nothing you can do for me now. At the time, perhaps I... But it is too late!'

The tragic look of the brown eyes in their golden setting, the note of despair in her voice, were more than Wyndham could bear. He lowered his tone to a murmur, leaning towards her.

'Miss Reeth—Serena—don't look like that, I beg of you! Whatever it is, I pledge you my word that I will do anything I can to aid you.'

'Oh, no, you must not!' she uttered, in a frantic undertone. 'Pray do not speak of it. Do not speak to me, if you can avoid it. You will only make everything worse.'

Wyndham heard these words with deep concern. That Serena was in trouble he could not doubt. It put a completely different construction upon the situation from that which he had intended. He had enlisted his cousin's aid to ensure Serena's attendance at the house party in a bid to rescue her from Hailcombe's importunities. Not that he had supposed that the fellow posed any serious threat. He thought better of Serena than to suppose her capable of succumbing to such a man. But his underlying reason had been to find an opportunity to reinstate himself in Serena's favour. He had hoped to tease her into submission, and find out—and if possible eradicate—whatever it might be that had caused her to draw away from him.

But her present distress could not wholly be attributed to her finding herself in his company. That she was in a serious difficulty he could not doubt, and he determined there and then to extricate her from it.

'We will talk of it tomorrow,' he said quietly. 'I will arrange it without any harm to you, I promise.'

With which, he turned from her and devoted himself to the lady on his other side, leaving Serena to the attentions of the elderly cleric, who had by now discovered the presence of what he termed 'the lovely young thing' beside him.

It was with mixed feelings that Serena joined a riding party consisting of the younger guests and the daughter of the house. Melanie had invaded Serena's bedchamber at an early hour, with a giggling brunette in tow, to inform her of the projected ride and demand her attendance.

'You must hurry, for we must needs ride before breakfast, or it will be hours before we can do so without unsettling our stomachs. Now, Serena, do not say that you have not brought your habit, because—'

'Of course I have brought it,' broke in Serena, still heavy with sleep, 'but I have no horse, Mel!'

A trill of laughter gushed out of her hostess, and her companion broke into giggles. Serena had been introduced to her last night after dinner as Lady Fanny Gullane, a schoolfriend of Melanie's. Serena thought her pretty, if a trifle empty-headed, and judged her a devotee and follower of her more ebullient friend.

'You don't need a horse, silly,' chided Melanie. 'We shall mount you, of course. Do you ride well? Not that it matters. I am sure George will not sanction any other horse than will give you a safe ride.'

'Oh, yes,' chimed in Lady Fanny, 'gentlemen will never be brought to believe that one can perfectly well hold a strong horse. Felix is forever cosseting me about with restrictions, and insists upon my riding a *well-mannered* filly.'

'Felix' was Lord Horsmonden, the very young gentleman to whom Lady Fanny had recently become betrothed. He had only just attained his majority, and though their attachment was of long standing an engagement had been delayed until now.

Fanny's remarks provoked a lively discussion between the two young ladies on the subject of the ridiculous shibboleths with which they claimed that their respective husbands-to-be incessantly plagued them. But as the mists of sleep receded, Serena's attention became fixed upon the implications inherent in the proposed riding scheme.

According to Melanie, it was the Viscount who had the mounting of Serena. His cousin was ready to grant him the authority that could only be his if Serena had accepted him. An assumption that could not but raise a seed of resentment inside her. Unless it was Wyndham's plan? Had he chosen this method of ensuring that promised tête-à-tête, the thought of which had kept her awake for hours?

She had little opportunity to dwell upon this question, for Melanie and her friend proceeded to harry her to get dressed, both taking it upon themselves to act in the capacity of lady's maid, which hindered rather than speeded Serena's progress. But at last she emerged from the bedchamber, clad in a habit of sky-blue that so enhanced her beauty as to make two of the three gentlemen awaiting them at the stables goggle with blatant admiration.

The third, whose eyes Serena's involuntarily sought, gave her a smile of welcome that shot her through with ripples of guilty yearning.

'Allow me to help you to mount,' he said, adding softly, 'You look enchanting!'

'Th-thank you.' Delight set her cheeks aglow.

Wyndham took her gloved hand in his, and led her towards a neat grey in the charge of one of the many grooms. Too flustered to notice that the Honourable John Camelford and Lord Horsmonden were performing the same office for their respective fiancées, Serena accepted his aid in silence.

Under cover of the general chatter as the party mounted up, Wyndham murmured, 'Thank you for coming. We will find an opportunity to converse.'

She was reaching for the reins, but she paused and the pansy eyes flew to his, so vulnerable an expression in her face that he was hard put to it to refrain from kissing it away.

'Up with you!' he said quickly, and threw her into the saddle.

Automatically, Serena arranged her leg and settled

herself, slipping her foot comfortably into the stirrup as Wyndham guided it through, and gathering up the reins. She was obliged to take in calming draughts of air, for his nearness, the intimacy of his tone, and the pressure of his hands upon her waist had thrown her pulses into utter disarray.

Her resolution was in shreds. To be treated to just those attentions she wanted from the man to whom she must not give her heart, and from whom she had been ordered to remain aloof, was completely demoralising. His proffered help—no, his promise of it!—was that forbidden balm which she had been given no opportunity to refuse. She must refuse it! If he did take the chance to talk to her in some degree of privacy, she was in honour bound to reject his every attempt to win her confidence.

The thought of that necessity so wrought upon her that it was through a blur that she saw the Viscount swing himself into the saddle, to bestride a monstrous chestnut that he controlled with ease. The others were already trotting out of the stableyard. Winking away the momentary weakness, Serena nodded to the groom still holding her horse, and started off behind them.

Wyndham fell in beside her, but at a discreet distance that precluded conversation for the moment. No words were exchanged while the party made its way across the Lacey estates to a bridle path that ran adjacent, and which led, so Melanie had informed her, to a stretch of open country where they might enjoy a gallop.

Serena had ample opportunity to discover that so far from insulting her horsemanship with the dull ride deemed suitable to a lady, the Viscount had chosen a spirited filly with a number of sportive tricks that kept Serena pretty well occupied for some time in bringing her to heel. She could not but be aware of Wyndham riding nearby, and guessed that he was ready to intervene at need. Ahead, the two other young ladies, who were riding with their heads together behind their menfolk leading the way, had also been mounted on cattle of quality.

There was ample time for her nerves to settle, along with those of her mount. By the time they came to the bridle path—where necessity compelled the Viscount to ride at her side—Serena was able to answer him with scarcely a tremor. Though she could not prevent the blood from flittering down her veins.

'My uncle, I am happy to say, is a shrewd judge of horseflesh,' Wyndham began, innocuously enough.

'I can see that.' Serena threw him a glance. 'Did you select this mount for me?'

His brows went up. 'Do you object?'

A tremor ran through her, but she answered with an assumption of calm. 'On the contrary, I am very grateful. Particularly as your cousin assured me that you were bound to choose a *safe* ride for me.'

'Mel wants sense as well as conduct,' he said, mock-severe. 'I make you her apologies.'

'Oh, pray don't. I like her very much. Indeed, I do not see how anyone could not, for she is so very warm-hearted.'

'Yes, which is why she is forgiven the all too frequent indiscretions of her tongue.'

He was treated to Serena's shy smile, and a glow suffused his chest. She was relaxing at last.

'I am scarcely in a position to condemn her there.'

Wyndham grinned at her. 'But in you, Miss Reeth, such indiscretions are a refreshment and a delight— as I believe I have had occasion to tell you in the past.'

Her cheeks flew colour, and she looked quickly away. 'It is a—a past, sir, that had better be forgotten.'

The constriction in her voice warned him to tread with care. Yet there it was again! The inexplicable withdrawal that had at first so enraged him. It had been only the realisation that Serena was struggling against her instinct—which he would swear to be in his favour!—that had assuaged his wrath and caused him to question the origin of the change she had exhibited towards him.

He knew better than to mention the matter directly. Nor was he prepared to probe the meaning of her allusion to the Marquis of Sywell. Besides, his need to absolve himself had been superseded by the trouble he had perceived in Serena last night. His mission was not at this present to reinstate himself—beyond winning back her trust—but to investigate the mystery of her evident distress.

Serena's voice jerked him out of his thoughts. It contained a note of accusation. And a thread of anger?

'It was you who arranged for me to be invited, was it not? Pray will you tell me why?'

'Because I wanted an opportunity to recover our former ease of friendship,' Wyndham said without hesitation.

She was silent, looking directly ahead, but there was a telltale stiffness in her shoulders. Dared he pursue it? What had he got to lose? Even if she grew angry, it would at least break down this intolerable barrier. And it must be broken, or he would get nowhere.

'Your father told me that you had transferred your affections to another. Which led me to conclude that I had at one time the good fortune to be the object of your affections. Forgive my bluntness, Miss Reeth, but you must know that it is still my earnest desire to attach you.'

'Oh, don't!' came from his companion in a stifled tone. 'Pray don't! I am not permitted... I mean, you cannot wish—I think you cannot wish to—to distress me with...'

'That, never!' he declared. 'But it seems to me that you are already distressed, Serena—and not on my account.'

Unable to help herself, Serena looked round at him. The sincerity of compassion in his face was all too convincing. How could he be the monster that had been painted for her? He was waiting for some sort of reply. It did not occur to Serena to withhold herself from making it.

'I am at outs with Papa, that is all.'

But the Viscount was not to be satisfied with this dismissive response. 'Upon what occasion? Nothing, I do trust, to do with my offer?'

'Oh, no. At least—not directly.'

Realising that she was being drawn to reveal more than she wished—or indeed ought!—Serena tried to put a curb upon her tongue. It was so difficult to obey Papa, especially when everything in her cried out to her to do precisely the opposite to his commandments.

'He—he did not wish me to leave town at this present,' she said, improvising desperately in a bid to depart from the dangerous truth. 'He is desirous of my—my doing something that I—that I—' Hunting her mind, she came up with a compromise. 'I am afraid I have rebelled against his express command, and—and I do not know how it is to be resolved.'

She would have been appalled had she an inkling that Wyndham experienced no difficulty in interpreting this halting prevarication. But then Serena was not to know that her recent movements had been reported to him by his closest friend.

Sebastian Moore, Lord Buckworth, was a man of much larger proportion than his crony, but who shared with him both a sense of humour and a natural aptitude for the skill of fencing. They were remarkably well matched, which discovery had been, some years ago, the origin of their friendship. Buckworth was somewhat older than the Viscount, and apt to treat him with the lazy amusement that characterised him. But he had been serious enough when he had

deduced that the female of his best friend's choice—
having summarily rejected Wyndham, much to
Buckworth's astonishment—was the unwilling object
of the advances of a man whose reputation had led to
his being largely ostracised by the *beau monde*.

'If I am any judge, dear boy,' had said Buckworth,
in a light tone laced with sympathy, 'it is the parent
rather than the girl who favours that fellow's suit.'

Buckworth had seen Serena in Hailcombe's company, both in the park and at the theatre, and had been
unable to discern the slightest sign in her either of
attachment or enjoyment. The duenna, on the other
hand, had been encouraging in the extreme. Which
had been surprising, if Buckworth had not seen Lord
Reeth and Hailcombe together on two separate occasions.

It was thus clear to Wyndham that the dispute between Serena and her father must have to do with
Hailcombe's suit. The discovery both incensed and
disgusted him. That Reeth could reject himself, with
the flimsy excuse that Serena no longer favoured him,
was bad enough. And now he came to think of it, had
not the man floundered in embarrassment when asked
to give a reason for his refusal? But then instead to
determine to give his daughter to a man like
Hailcombe! It was beyond either belief or reason.

A hail from his cousin informed Wyndham that
they were approaching the open country. Another moment, and the opportunity for private speech would
be lost.

He looked at Serena, and found her studying his

face, a frown creasing her brow. Wyndham smiled at her.

'I thank you for your confidence, Miss Reeth. We will talk again later.'

Uneasily aware of having betrayed far more than she intended, Serena rode out into the open in a mood of silent anxiety. But the exhilaration of a gallop succeeded in driving away the cobwebs in her mind, if only temporarily.

The six horses flew across the turf, kicking up mud and grasses, their riders easy in the saddle, at one with the rhythmic rise and fall engendered by the speeding hooves. In a short space of time, Serena had reason to be grateful for the Viscount's choice, for the filly rapidly outstripped the mounts of the other two ladies, racing neck and neck with the big chestnut. Aware that Wyndham was holding in his horse in order to stay with her, Serena reined in to a canter.

'Give him his head! I will await you. Don't fear for me, for I will not gallop again when you are not by.'

A salute of his whip thanked her, and the chestnut streaked ahead. Serena heard a tally-ho behind her, and turned her head to see that the other two gentlemen were following this lead. Drawing her own mount in, she let them pass, and dropped to a walk, in which she was soon joined by the other two young ladies.

'Well, I wouldn't have thought it of George!' exclaimed Melanie crossly. 'Bad enough for Camel to have deserted me, but I never suspected Wyndham could be so selfish!'

'Oh, do not say so!' cried Serena, dismayed. 'I told him to go, for I could see his mount was itching for a proper run. And he is much stronger than this little lady.'

'Oh, well, I dare say there is no harm done then,' said Melanie merrily. 'To tell the truth, it is tedious to be forever subject to Camel's strictures and instruction.'

'Yes, and only see how comfortable a cose we may have without them all,' agreed Lady Fanny. 'We may abuse them to our heart's content.'

Serena had no wish to abuse the Viscount, but she had no need to say so, for the other two girls instantly embarked upon a laughing discussion of the faults of their hapless heroes, which proceeded without any assistance from her. Wistfully, she thought how little they both had real cause to complain. It was obvious that both John Camelford and Lord Horsmonden were gentlemen of amiable disposition. Serena could not suppose that either would turn out to have been corrupted by a horrible marquis! Nor did she think that either lady was filled with disgust at the thought of her coming marriage.

Her spirits dropped with the remembrance of Hailcombe. Somehow, while she permitted herself the guilty indulgence of partaking of Wyndham's company, it seemed to Serena the more inevitable that she would find herself forced to accede to Papa's demand.

All very well to stand out against her father, but for how long could she continue to do so?

She watched Wyndham riding back towards her. In an ideal world, she might have been awaiting the return of her betrothed, just as the other two females were doing. But the world—alas!—was far from ideal, and it was foolish to indulge in useless dreams.

Upon the thought, a swell of emotion rose within her, and she felt unequal to any further exchange with his lordship. Turning her mount before he could reach her, Serena encouraged the grey to break into a canter. She did not look round when Wyndham's chestnut appeared to one side, and deliberately ignored his call to her to wait.

But Serena reckoned without her host. Wyndham came in close and seized her rein, bringing both horses to a halt. A rush of sudden anger superseded Serena's distress.

'What the devil is amiss, Serena?' he demanded, a touch of irritation in his voice. 'But a few moments since I thought we had come to an understanding.'

Serena perforce turned her head and met his eyes. Her voice was pitched low and tense. 'Pray let go my rein!'

'I will do so when you answer me.'

Her breath caught in her chest and speech became painful. But there was no stopping the words from coming out.

'There can be no understanding between us, Wyndham. Every moment I allow you to draw me in, I am compounding my fault.'

'I am trying to help you, not to draw you in.'

'You cannot help me. You, of all people. I am not even supposed to talk to you!'

Wyndham's gaze narrowed. 'Is that your father's command?'

Serena looked him straight in the eyes. 'And my own determination.'

There was silence for a moment. He was holding her gaze, and pain gathered at her heart as she saw the grey eyes grow steely. His voice was no less chilling for its quiet.

'You mentioned once the name of a certain marquis. I do not know what you may have been told to my discredit in this connection. But it wounds me, Serena, that our acquaintance has resulted in you knowing me so little.'

With which he released his hold on her rein and, sharply turning his horse, rode a little away and stopped. With an ironic gesture he invited her to precede him towards the others who had ridden on ahead and were moving towards the entrance to the bridle path.

Having excused herself, on the score of an abdominal pain, from joining an excursion to a neighbouring estate for a morning assembly, Serena had watched the carriages depart, and then donned her green pelisse and taken her misery out of doors.

Cousin Laura was safely ensconced in a downstairs parlour, whither she had told her charge she would hide herself for the purpose of writing a long overdue letter to her friend, Miss Lucinda Beattie of Abbot Giles. The mention of that name, bringing to the fore the painful origin of Serena's unhappiness, had been enough to cause an escalation of her feelings that could not but result in a hearty bout of weeping.

A number of little summerhouses dotted the grounds of Lacey Court. Together with innumerable other grottoes, mazes and sunken gardens, these formed part of the extravagant landscaping and ornamentation created during the last century.

Concealed in one of these, Serena was finally able to release the dammed up well of emotion that had plagued her. How she had borne her part in the gaiety exhibited by the other young people, she did not know. She could only marvel that it was not apparent to others that my Lord Wyndham contrived to address only the merest commonplace to Miss Reeth, at moments when common courtesy demanded it.

There was a complete absence of the teasing look and the warm smile, and Serena knew she ought to have been grateful that it had been made easy for her to obey Papa's command. But she could only feel desperately hurt. If Wyndham had been wounded by her belief of his guilt, then he was wonderfully revenged!

Worse was the realisation forced upon Serena of the hope she had been secretly nursing. The Viscount had given her to understand that he still wanted to marry her; that he would help her if he could. In honour bound, she had rejected both sentiments. But their withdrawal seemed to seal her doom.

She would have to give in to Papa. What alternative had she? She could not even think of one of the other gentlemen who had admired her in the past. Lord Reeth's determination was fixed upon Hailcombe. And indeed, she decided dismally, if she could not marry Wyndham, it mattered little whom she married, for all hope of happiness was blighted for ever.

Upon this melancholy thought, a fresh deluge of tears coursed down her cheeks. Serena dabbed ineffectually at them with her drenched pockethandkerchief, which had long since proved to be inadequate to the level of her woe.

'Take mine,' said a voice from nowhere, causing Serena's heart to jerk with a violence that stopped the flow of tears in its tracks.

Her startled gaze beheld Wyndham, hatless, one booted foot upon the little step that led into the summerhouse, leaning towards her and holding out a pristine white handkerchief.

'You made me nearly jump out of my skin!' she cried involuntarily, seizing the handkerchief without thought as a pounding started up in her chest.

He looked rueful. 'I beg your pardon. I have been watching you for some little time, and there did not seem to be a propitious moment for declaring my presence.'

'You should have declared it!' returned Serena, snapping uncontrollably as she attempted to repair the ravages that her emotions had wrought upon her countenance.

Hideously aware that her eyes must be swollen, her

nose red, her cheeks disgracefully patchy and her hair awry, she tried to turn in a bid to avoid his glance. But the round summerhouse, with its iron fretwork columns, was so tiny as to permit the half-circle that formed the little seat—built, one could not deny, for the comfort of two persons only—to offer no protection.

'Don't turn away from me!' begged Wyndham, stepping up so that he seemed to fill the restricted space.

She was dismayed. 'Oh, no—you must not! Pray go away again, sir!'

'By no means,' he said, placing himself beside her on the narrow seat, and possessing himself of one of her hands. 'I cannot leave you in such distress. Especially since I cannot rid myself of the conviction that I have contributed to it.'

In no small degree! But it would not do for him to know it. She tried to pull her fingers out of his hold, a trifle breathless for the chaos of her pulses.

'Pray l-let me go! It has—it is not—I am not crying for anything that you have done.'

Wyndham retained his hold on her hand. 'You might well, however. I am palpably to blame for taking unnecessary offence the other day. I gave you my word that I would help you, and then deserted you. I can only beg you to forgive me.'

These words, coupled with the disturbing touch of his fingers, could not but offer balm to Serena's bruised spirit. But a part of her rose up in obstinate

defiance, and the words came unbidden from her
mouth. She snatched her hand away.

'Why should I forgive you? You had me brought
here for—for purposes of your own. You probed my
secrets from me, though I told you I cannot accept
your help. And then you must needs taunt me with—
with judging you, when I have tried not to do so. And
I cannot find out the truth, for I am not permitted to
ask you about it, because females must not know of
such things!'

Realising belatedly where her tongue was leading
her, Serena stopped with a gasp, and made to leap
from the seat. A strong hand prevented her, dragging
her back again.

'Now you listen to me!' said Wyndham firmly,
pulling her round to face him. 'I neither know nor
care what stories may have been told to you, my girl,
but I will not tolerate these insults. What I am or what
I may have done in the past is not your concern! Had
you accepted my suit, and found my conduct wanting
in the future, you might have cause to complain. As
things stand—'

This was not to be borne. Serena's temper flared.
Seizing his wrists, she wrenched his hands off her
shoulders.

'How dare you speak to me in this fashion? I had
no idea how horrid you can be! I thought you kind
and gentle, and now I see how mistaken I have been.'

'For the matter of that,' retorted Wyndham, 'I
thought you a charming innocent. Little did I know

how shrewish a temper lurked inside that pretty façade!'

'Then you cannot be other than glad that Papa refused to allow me to marry you!'

Jumping up, Serena stepped quickly out of the summerhouse. But she had hardly gone a few hasty yards in the direction of the house, when Wyndham was once more beside her, catching at her hand.

'Stop! Serena, don't run away!'

Before she knew what he would be at, he had turned her to him, and his fingers were cupping her face, while one hand snaked up to stroke her golden hair. His eyes were alight with warmth and remorse. Serena's furious resentment died, and her pulses pattered into life.

'Forgive me, for I did not mean it. I have been unreasonable, have I not? If I am permitted an excuse, let it be that my disappointment has made me subject to unhappy changes of temperament.'

At these words, which contained the empty promise of that fulfilment of her deepest desires, all Serena's earlier misery welled up again, and she spoke her heart aloud.

'If you are disappointed, how much greater must be my unhappiness in the choice that has been made for me.'

Her voice failed, and she saw Wyndham's expression change.

'Oh, don't weep!'

His fingers left her face, and Serena found herself caught into an alarming embrace, his encircling arms bringing her so close that she could feel his limbs against her own. A trembling started up inside her, and a sensation of lightness invaded her head.

Wyndham held her so for a moment, looking down into her face. In some dim corner of Serena's brain, she knew she ought to release herself. But she could not have moved if she had wanted to. Mesmerised, her eyes locked with his.

'My sweet Serena,' he murmured. 'So very beautiful. And so innocent, God help me!'

And then his lips came down on hers, his eyes closing. The touch was featherlight. Serena felt her knees go weak and the feeling of light-headedness increased. Into her mind floated a random thought. This was how it ought to have been—after her betrothal. Only she was not betrothed to Wyndham.

Her eyes flew open, and she pulled back in instinctive reaction, staggering as the support of his arms gave way.

'You kissed me!' she accused stupidly.

Wyndham was unable to help a shaky laugh. 'Yes, I'm afraid I did.'

'You had no right to kiss me.'

A vision leapt into her mind. Wyndham—kissing other females. Women whose class permitted such licence.

'No right—save that of my need of you,' he said. 'And that is very real!'

The next instant, Serena found herself locked in an embrace more powerful than the first. Wyndham's mouth sought hers again. Not gently at all, but roughly, with a pressure that forced her lips apart. Instinctively, Serena knew that this second kiss was dictated by passion.

But the thought was swiftly drowned by an impression that she was bursting into flame as the power of his assault upon her mouth intensified. Her own violent reaction sent her into panic. Struggling, she fought to be free.

Recollecting himself suddenly, Wyndham let her go. She reeled back, the brown eyes gazing at him in mute horror. He put out an unsteady hand.

'Serena—I beg your pardon! I forgot myself.'

But the apology came too late. She put her fingers to her mouth, touching her lips as if to assure herself they were not injured. She was shaking uncontrollably, her voice hoarse.

'How could you, Wyndham? Oh, how *could* you!'

Turning, she fled from him, her faith in him shattered.

Chapter Five

The Reeth coach drew slowly away from the environs of the Lacey estate. Cousin Laura, who had been leaning forward to look out of the window, now sank back against the squabs, turning with a sigh towards Serena.

'I have so enjoyed this little trip. What a pity you chose to come away a day early, my dear. Now you will have no young companions for your outings.'

'It makes no matter,' said Serena listlessly, for she no longer cared whether or not she had company. She anticipated no pleasure in any outing, and would as lief stay at home.

'I cannot conceive why you wished to leave,' pursued her duenna, fiddling with the dull grey cloak she wore. A trifle of peevishness crept into her voice. 'There was plenty of amusement, and you have learned to hold Wyndham at arm's length, so that—'

'I beg you will not mention that name to me again, cousin!' flared Serena. 'If at one time I thought well of his lordship, that is all at an end.'

She was dismayed to see that Cousin Laura peered closely at her in the relative gloom of the carriage, and hastily turned her face towards the window. For no consideration would she discuss the circumstances that had led to the realisation that Papa had spoken nothing but the truth. Else Wyndham would not have treated her to a smouldering embrace that ought better have been reserved for the women of that class whose business it was to receive such caresses.

That her memory of the dreadful event had a curious power to make her go weak at the knees was but a blacker mark against him. He had no right to make her feel as if her bones had been filleted! But that was not the worst. Until he had kissed her in that deplorable fashion, Serena had thought him too gentlemanlike to have been guilty of the sort of conduct of which Cousin Laura accused him. Now she knew her partiality had been mistaken.

Worse yet, Wyndham had categorically stated that his way of life before he met her was no concern of hers. Which served only to convince her that, in his eyes, those shocking activities indulged in with the Marquis of Sywell were merely the peccadilloes which Cousin Laura had said might be forgiven.

Recalling how the Viscount had told her he was wounded by her judgement of him, Serena could only marvel. Could he not see how his licentious conduct must give her a disgust of him? He had so often spoken of her as innocent, yet he believed that she ought to condone it. Or, at the least, ignore it.

Serena had been made to understand that, despite

her misplaced feeling for Wyndham, they were poles apart. Papa had been right all along. All hope of happiness was thus at an end, and love was dead.

She realised that Cousin Laura was speaking, and tried to concentrate. She could understand her duenna's disappointment in leaving Lacey Court, for she'd had little need of chaperonage and Cousin Laura had been free, for once in her life, to pursue her own interests.

'I believe I have read as many as three novels, for Lady Lacey has an excellent collection. And I have discovered that Lady Camelford enjoys a game of chess, which as you know is one of my accomplishments, thanks to my Reverend Papa's teaching. We had several bouts, and I must confess myself to have been delighted to beat Lady Camelford twice more than she beat me.'

Serena wished she might share Cousin Laura's enthusiasm. But the truth was that, although she had played her part in the various entertainments got up amongst the younger set, and had tried to emulate Mel's enthusiasm—more for the purpose of showing Lord Wyndham that she could very well get on without him than anything else!—Serena had been too sick at heart to enjoy anything. After two days, she had grown weary of feigning, and found an excuse to take her departure on Wednesday, a day earlier than the rest of the party.

Not that Melanie had believed her fabrication! Serena had complained of increasing pain and nausea at her stomach, and refused all offers to send for the local doctor.

'I do not wish him—that is, *people*—' correcting herself hastily '—to suppose that I am unwell. It will only spoil the party.'

'But if you go early, Serena,' Melanie had pointed out with alarming candour, 'these "people" are bound to think that something is amiss. What am I supposed to tell *them*?'

The stress laid on the final word had warned Serena that her subterfuge had been detected. Refusing to acknowledge it, she had persisted in her determination.

'Once I am gone, you may say what you please.'

'And what reason do you propose to give before you are gone?' had demanded Melanie.

Serena had sighed. 'Oh, we shall say that I have a recurrent disorder that forces me to return to London to consult my physician. He is familiar with my case, you see.'

'Yes, and if you ask me, there is a great deal more to your "case" than a pain at the stomach!'

Which percipient remark had almost been Serena's undoing. But Melanie was as warm-hearted as she was loose-tongued, and had given her guest a quick hug.

'There, don't cry! You shall go if you choose. Only pray don't try to bamboozle me into believing that George has not upset you, for you will not succeed. If I could think it might do some good, I would take him roundly to task!'

'Oh, pray do not!' had begged Serena, alarmed.

'No, I shan't, for he wouldn't listen to me if I did,' had said Melanie frankly. 'I should think Buckworth is the only person who has influence with George, and his advice is unlikely to be of the least use.'

With which sentiment Serena found herself to be in full agreement. Indeed, she must suppose that a rake, as Buckworth had been described to her, could only encourage that side of Wyndham to which she fervently wished she had herself remained a stranger. An uncomfortable reflection that had sunk her below melancholy into the apathy that now engulfed her. For there was only one future for her, and she had determined to school herself to endure it.

The Viscount's attention was so distracted that, for the second time at practice, he foolishly allowed a simple pass to break through his guard. Buckworth leaped back out of range and dropped his point.

'A child's trick, Wyndham, and you let me through! You are not concentrating. *En garde!*'

The mock fight resumed, and Wyndham, always on the defensive, parried almost mechanically, for his mind continued to run on the difficulties of his situation.

Once Serena had left the Lacey Court party, it had proved abominably insipid—despite the fact that she had virtually ignored him for the last two days. He had tried to convince himself that he had been wasting his time. It was not his business to sort out Miss

Reeth's life. He was out of the running, and she could well manage her affairs for herself.

But he'd had glimpses of her during this past week since his return to town, and had caught himself out in a high tide of jealousy on seeing Hailcombe assiduously at her elbow. He had forced his attention on to his own plans, for he was due to go to Brighton in a day or so. Custom dictated that gentlemen of the Ton followed the Prince, who had already left the metropolis to spend time there with his particular cronies.

Wyndham was just reflecting that Brighton held no lure for him at this present, when it was borne in upon him that Buckworth was attempting a lunge *in quarte*, high to the shoulder. Too late, he fumbled a parry, and his friend's buttoned point came to rest upon his left breast.

'*Touché*,' he acknowledged, and stepped back.

'No credit to me,' Buckworth pointed out, putting up a hand to remove the mask from his face. 'Your guard was weak, and you know it.'

'True.' With a sigh, Wyndham removed his own mask. 'I have had enough, in any event.'

'What's amiss, dear boy?' asked Buckworth, taking his friend's foil and placing both back in the rack.

Wyndham answered only with a grunt, handed his mask to one of the attendants, and headed for the washroom. Buckworth had better have asked what was not amiss! How could one begin to tell him? That he had been a fool? But that went without saying. He had been precipitate, ungentlemanly, and above all, he had lost control. And it had cost him dear.

A large arm was placed about his shoulders, and he found Buckworth at his side.

'Come on, man, out with it! It's the little Reeth creature, I take it?'

Wyndham looked quickly about, but the washroom was deserted. Most of the fellows who frequented Angelo's academy must be still at practice in the long room set aside for the purpose.

'As you say,' he said lightly.

Moving out of his friend's embrace, he went to a stand and, lifting the ewer, poured water into the basin.

'I'm not going to leave it, my friend,' said Buckworth, following suit at another stand, 'so you may as well cut line.'

'The thing is,' confessed Wyndham, taking off his shirt and throwing water over himself, 'that I don't know where to start. I've made a mull of it, I can tell you that.'

'That much I had already deduced,' said his friend. 'I've never yet met a man who was blue-devilled in affairs of the heart who hadn't done his best to shoot himself in the foot!'

Wyndham gave a short laugh, and picked up the soap. In a few pithy words, he put his friend in possession of the salient facts. He did not spare himself, for it was much needed balm to be able to throw off the social mask with this friend whom he trusted above all others.

'I should have known better,' he said bitterly at the end of his recital. 'She's only eighteen.'

'That means nothing at all, George. I've known girls of eighteen who wouldn't turn a hair. It all depends on the upbringing.'

'Reeth is very strict, I believe. And she is childishly innocent. Her conversation is enough to tell one that. Lord knows what sort of a fairytale he concocted for her benefit! And just when I thought I had succeeded in convincing her otherwise—'

Breaking off, Wyndham ground his teeth, feeling a resurgence of all the useless fury he had expended against himself. That Serena had been frightened by his kiss into withdrawal, he knew. That she now regarded him with revulsion, he could not doubt. And he was almost certain that she had decided to believe whatever tales had been told of him to put her against him. Couple that with the prohibitions that her father had evidently laid upon her, and the Viscount must conceive his case to be hopeless.

He looked at Buckworth, who was vigorously rubbing himself with a towel, and found an amused gaze upon him.

'And what, may I ask, do you find so devilishly funny?' he demanded. 'My life is in ruins, and all you can do is laugh!'

Buckworth grinned at him, and threw him one of the towels that hung on a convenient rail. 'I always thought you would take it badly when it hit.'

'When what hit?'

'Love.'

Arrested, Wyndham paused with the towel draped about his bare shoulders. He regarded the twinkling eyes of his friend without annoyance, for the significance in that one word took all his attention. It struck him that in all his dealings on this matter, he had never admitted the truth.

Having been dismissed by Reeth, he had wanted to wash his hands of the whole affair. But that had proved impossible. For there had been Serena—distressed from the outset!—and he had been unable to leave it alone. He had thought it was her difficulties and tribulations that had been driving him. Had he been deceiving himself all this while?

'Lord, Buckworth!' he uttered dazedly. 'I am so very deeply in love with her. What the devil am I to do?'

October was almost at an end, and the lonely week since Serena had departed from the house party at Lacey Court felt like a lifetime. Hailcombe had been her escort at almost every engagement she had attended, and she had been made aware—by Cousin Laura, who spoke of it with satisfaction—that the announcement of her betrothal was daily expected.

Serena had not herself noticed the whispers, for she had been living in a hazy world where nothing seemed any longer to be real. Her speech and actions were mechanical, and she could not remember what had been said to her five minutes after a conversation.

Only one thing penetrated the cloud of abstraction in which she had enwrapped herself. Despite every determination to cut a certain unmentionable gentleman out of her life and memory, it was upon the three separate occasions when she discovered him to be present at the same event she was attending that a piercing pang shot her into a state of mental alertness.

Serena's remembrance of the week behind her jumped from one to the other of these unfortunate encounters. The difficulty, she discovered, was that Wyndham was as personable as ever, and had yet the smile and warmth that characterised him—if not towards herself. He should, she felt, have grown horns and a tail, and shown his evil propensities in some harsh transformation of his countenance! It was really too bad of him to hide his true identity under that engaging personality which had captured her fancy. It was all of a piece, and just the hypocritical conduct one might have expected.

These damaging reflections, however, failed to cure Serena of her depressed spirits. Indeed, they had an opposite effect, and her wan looks at length drew her duenna's expostulation.

'My dear child, anyone would suppose you to be at death's door! Do try to show a little animation. It is of particular importance this morning, for Hailcombe is coming to see your Papa and I have no doubt you will be expected to attend him.'

Serena was vaguely aware that there was significance in this announcement. 'I thought we were with him last night at the Opera. Am I engaged to drive out with him?'

Cousin Laura was moved to click her tongue, shuffling her spectacles on and off again. 'I do wish you will come out of this stupid dullness, Serena! Surely you heard him say last night that he would call upon your Papa this morning? You must have done so, for you readily agreed that it was convenient.'

No recollection of having said any such thing came into Serena's head. But then last night had been a severe trial to her, for the Viscount had been in a box on the other side of the opera house. Had it been his aunt, Lady Lacey, with him? She rather thought it had, but she could not be sure, for her gaze had been strictly confined to the stage. Not that it had helped. She'd had no notion how large an arc was encompassed in the periphery of one's vision! Nor how obtrusive upon it could be a single figure at a distance.

A knock at the nursery parlour door produced Lissett. 'His lordship requests you to join him in the library, Miss Serena.'

Serena looked at him blankly. 'Do you mean Lord Hailcombe?'

'Lord Hailcombe is in the first-floor saloon. It is my Lord Reeth who wishes your presence in the book-room.'

'Very well, I will come.'

The butler withdrew, and Serena rose from her chair, only to be checked by Cousin Laura.

'One moment, child.' Her duenna twitched at the demure muslin gown, and prinked the golden curls. 'There, that will suffice. Now, Serena, you are going to do your duty, are you not? It will not do to turn tail at this juncture.'

Serena fought down a sudden disquieting nausea. 'I am quite ready, cousin.'

Her duenna gave her a doubtful look, but turned to escort her along the corridor and downstairs to the library. Opening the door, she gave her charge a little push that precipitated her into the room.

Lord Reeth was standing before the fireplace, gripping the mantel. The bronzed head turned, and the Roman nose was directed towards his daughter. There was question in his lordship's gaze, and a riffle of feeling disturbed Serena's comforting blanket of unreality.

'You wanted to see me, Papa?'

For a moment, her father continued to regard her silently, as if he sought to satisfy himself upon certain points in his mind. The appraisal proved disconcerting, and Serena dropped her eyes.

'I do not know, Serena,' began Reeth at length, in that heavy tone which caused an uncomfortable sinking within his daughter's stomach, 'what may have occurred at Lacey Court to effect this change in you. Laura assures me that you are now schooled to obedience. I can only trust that this will be found to be the case.'

Serena's head continued downcast. Like a schoolgirl, she clasped her hands together behind her back, and closed her lips upon utterance. There was nothing to be said.

'Lord Hailcombe,' continued her father after a pause, 'has chosen to be magnanimous, and forgive the insulting nature of your earlier dealings with him.

He tells me that he has received nothing from you lately but that docility which must, he is persuaded, form the foundation of the sort of alliance that he desires.' The voice sharpened. 'In other words, Serena, he wishes for a wife who knows her duty and from whom he may expect obedience.'

There was a further dilution of the grey clouds about Serena's mind. With it arose a growth of sensation which was faintly reminiscent of the first occasion when she had been told of Hailcombe's offer. Serena kept her gaze lowered, apprehensive lest Papa's discerning eye should penetrate into the secret hollows of her bosom.

'You have nothing to say?'

There was scepticism in the voice. Serena drew a breath against the slight rise of panic, and looked up.

'What do you want me to say, Papa?'

'Good God, girl, don't you know? Don't think I have not observed you closely. I see you apparently cowed, but I am forced to wonder. I know you, Serena, and this conduct is not in your nature. What are you playing at?'

Hurt surprise jerked Serena into speech. 'Indeed, Papa, I do not know what you mean! I am ready to do as you ask. I made up my mind to it some time ago.'

Reeth frowned doubtfully. 'You will accept Hailcombe?'

'If that is your wish,' she agreed.

Papa seemed not to be satisfied. 'I warn you,

Serena, that if you again give me cause for embarrassment in this matter, I will not spare you!'

The meaning of this was plain. The remnants of the protective shroud in Serena's mind shredded away. Fully aware, she felt her heart knock against her ribs. A recognition that the fate outlined need not overtake her crept into her thoughts. She had every intention of obeying him. There was nothing to fear in Papa's veiled threat.

'You need not have said as much,' she said reproachfully. 'I have given you my word.'

Lord Reeth was unimpressed. 'Then see that you keep it!'

He strode past her to the door, and flung it open. Turning, Serena saw that her duenna was waiting in the corridor.

'Take her to the saloon, Laura. But wait outside. You had better let her face him alone.'

Hailcombe was standing behind one of the straw-covered sofas, his attention absorbed by something in the square below. Serena felt an upsurge of nausea. But her resolution, she reminded herself, was fixed. She trod silently to the centre of the saloon. The door clicked shut behind her.

His lordship turned his head, and Serena saw a frown in his eyes. His full mouth was tight-lipped in the florid features. It was not, Serena told herself, a bad-looking countenance. Well-proportioned with a strong jaw. If only the brows were not so heavy, and his smile had been engaging.

Was it a smile? He was showing his teeth, but there was no gleam of warmth at his eyes. They were grey, like Wyndham's. Only so unlike!

Serena's breath caught. Why had she thought of him? That was just the sort of comparison that must not enter her head. Feeling her control slipping, Serena dropped her gaze from his, and made her curtsey.

'You wished to see me, sir?'

Hailcombe came around the sofa and strolled to stand before the fireplace, at a little distance from her.

'Look at me, girl!'

It was a command. Something jolted in Serena's breast, but she obeyed, lifting her eyes again. She could not but note an arrogance in Hailcombe's pose, and with the lifted chin, the smile became a mocking sneer.

'Are you done rebelling?'

Serena knew not how to answer. Was he seeking to know if his way was clear, or was this to taunt her? It struck her that, for all the flaccidity of his frame, there was power in its very largeness. At her silence, the mockery intensified.

'Don't think me jealous. You're very young, and the young are wayward. Given time, I thought you'd come round.'

No longer sheltered by the numbness that had kept her docile, Serena was provoked into retort.

'My alteration, sir, had nothing to do with you!'

Hailcombe laughed. 'D'you think I care for that, if the prize be mine?'

Had she not schooled herself to accept this fate, Serena would have repudiated this assumption. She clamped her lips upon a rise of revulsion. But was there no ardour here? Had it been all pretence? Then why did he wish to marry her? She found a compromise of words.

'You presume it to be so, sir.'

'I think I may, don't you? You've behaved well to me these last days. Caused me to hope.'

Had she not intended this result? Then why should she feel so ill? Unable to answer, she dropped another curtsey, as if in acquiescence.

'Oh, that's submissive!' A smug satisfaction in his voice added nothing to Serena's comfort. 'Augurs well for our future together, Miss Reeth. Or might I use your pretty name now—eh, Serena?'

He came away from the mantel, and took a couple of paces towards her. 'I'm running before the horse, though. Let's do the thing in form.'

He made an elaborate, if clumsy, leg, and Serena could not tell whether he meant it in seriousness or mockery.

'Miss Reeth, will you honour me with your hand in marriage?'

A hard weight of denial settled squarely in Serena's chest. She knew it behoved her to speak, but her tongue refused to utter the necessary words. She swallowed hard, taking refuge in a further curtsey. Let him take that for his answer, for she could give him no other!

It appeared that Lord Hailcombe was all too willing

to take her answer as read. He came forward until he towered over her. Serena shrank into herself, and the sensation of sickness grew stronger. Under the thick brows his eyes looked down into her face with hardness in them, though his mouth smiled.

'By my faith, you're as pretty as a picture!' He chucked her under the chin. 'Made my path proverbially rough, but I won't repine. You can call me a happy man!'

Above her, the full lips protruded, the skin about them glistening. Before Serena had time to take in what he would be at, Hailcombe's hands were grasping her shoulders, and his face came down to the level of her own.

The next instant, a moist slab of rubbery flesh was fastened to her mouth, and a thrusting invader came oiling between her lips.

For several hideous seconds, the stark horror of the attack held Serena motionless, her limbs turning rigid. Then her stomach heaved, and an urgent need gave her strength. Recoiling, she tugged herself free.

With the back of her hand she wiped away the obscenity of his kiss, and her tongue gave utterance to the sensations consuming her.

'It is of no use! How can I marry you? *You repel me.*'

Turning from him, Serena ran for the door, brushing past her startled duenna. Clapping her hand over her mouth, she lifted her skirts, and flew up the stairs, racing for her bedchamber, convinced that at any moment she would regurgitate the churning contents of her stomach.

The furious banging on the door had abated. Papa's irate demands to Serena to come out had given way to a low-toned conversation in the corridor. Since she had—not without considerable difficulty—dragged the heavy oak chest across the locked door, and placed upon it a further barricade consisting of her bedside table and two straight-backed chairs, Serena was unable to approach close enough to place her ear to the woodwork—even had her trembling limbs permitted it. She could not therefore hear what was being said, but she knew that the participants consisted of her father, her duenna and the object of her violent rejection.

She was quivering still from the tirade that had been unleashed from the other side of the door. Papa's fury had known no bounds, and Serena had reason to congratulate herself on the quaking forethought that had led her to turn the key upon his inevitable revenge. In the appalling state of her nerves as she had fled for this refuge, it had been all she could do to slam the door and lock it before running for the washstand. In her frantic haste, she had dropped the ewer—mercifully empty!—and seized the basin in both hands.

She had not been sick, but the nausea continued to rise up from time to time. The basin was now on the bed where she had sat for several earth-shattering minutes, holding it ready, while her heaving interior made her retch over and over again.

And then had come the heavy footsteps of pursuit. At the first knock, and the demanding shout, Serena had staggered from the bed and stood, shivering with fright.

'Serena, open this door!'

The command was repeated several times. But so far from doing anything of the kind, Papa's erring daughter, driven to desperate measures by the vivid memory of his earlier promise, had well nigh exhausted herself in piling up her barrier.

'Call someone to break it down, Laura!'

But her duenna, to Serena's thankful ears, had vetoed this suggestion in no uncertain terms.

'Pray do not resort to ridiculous extremes, Bernard! She cannot remain in there for ever. You have only to have patience.'

'*Patience?* I'll show her patience!'

This outrage had been the prelude to a burst of invective and threatening language, accompanied by a thundering battery of fists upon the door. By the time Papa had run out of steam, Serena found herself backed into the opposite wall, with the bed between herself and the door, almost as if she would climb inside the stonework for protection.

She was able now to discern Hailcombe's voice as well as Cousin Laura's, in between the growling mutterings of Papa. But the words were indistinct. Eventually, the voices trailed away, and footsteps indicated that the party was moving off.

Serena's legs gave way and she sank into a huddle at the base of the wall, feeling numbed. For what felt like an age, she was unable to move from the spot, as the realisation of what had happened began to seep into her brain. With it, came a riot of conjecture.

How had she ever supposed she could ally herself with that creature? Yet how was she to escape him? What was she to do? Cousin Laura had spoken nothing but the truth. She could not stay here for ever. Would Papa's wrath be any more lenient for having grown cold? Retribution must await her, however long she held out. Hold out she must, for she would rather die than marry Hailcombe! How loathsome had been that kiss! Was she to endure a lifetime of revulsion? Better by far that she threw herself from the window of this room!

But the absurdity of this notion caught at her reason. No, that was foolish. Death was no solution. She must not fall into a distempered freak. Better to think how she could placate Papa, how to prevail upon him to realise the sheer impossibility of acceding to his wish.

A mountain loomed ahead of her. Involuntarily, she sighed aloud the root of the evil.

'Oh, Wyndham! If only you had not been a libertine!'

A memory shot into her mind. That kiss of his! It had shocked and alarmed her. But how unlike it had been to the hateful unpleasantness of Hailcombe's mouth upon her own. No such flame of heat had coursed through her as it had done upon the touch of

Wyndham's lips to hers. Had she to face again *his* arms about her, *his* assault upon her innocence, she had rather that a thousand times than to endure a single instant in the embrace of Hailcombe!

But that choice was not open to her, Serena reflected dismally, and dragging herself up from the floor, she drooped on to the bed. Faintness overcame her, and she lay down upon the coverlet, closing her eyes.

Exhaustion presently claimed her, and she knew no more until a gentle tapping on the door jerked her into wakefulness again. Starting up, and forgetful at first of the circumstances which had led to her being closeted in her bedchamber, Serena called out to know who was there.

'It is Mel. Dear Serena, do pray open the door!'

Bewildered, Serena stared blankly at the barricade. What in the world was Melanie doing here? And why was she lying upon her bed in the middle of the day?

It was a moment or two before remembrance came to her, and she recalled why the chest and other items were barring the doorway. By the time she had risen unsteadily to her feet and begun to cross the room, Melanie was again speaking.

'Serena, do you hear me? Pray come out! I have Miss Geary here, and she thinks you should come home with me for the night.'

Reaching the door, Serena took in the sense of these words with an abrupt rise of hope. But she was all too wary. Was this a trap?

'Mel? Is it indeed you?'

'Of course it is! Mama and I are in town for a few days for the purpose of ordering my bride clothes. But no matter for that. Pray let me help you, dearest Serena. You cannot remain in there indefinitely. Besides, you will soon be starving, and there is no bearing that.'

This aspect of the matter had not before occurred to Serena. But she now became aware that the nausea with which she had gone to sleep had given way to the pangs of hunger. Nevertheless, it was essential to proceed with caution.

'Cousin Laura?'

'My poor dear child,' came her duenna's anxious voice. 'You need have no fear. Your papa is out of the house. Come, Serena, open the door.'

'And Hailcombe? Is he here?'

'Dear me, no. He retreated in no small degree of umbrage several hours ago.'

Melanie took up the plea again. 'Serena, I do not know what has been happening here, but you will be safe at my home, I promise you.'

It took some further argument, but at length Serena allowed herself to be persuaded. Struggling, she undid her barricade, heaving the chest to one side. Unlocking the door, she opened it with a degree of stealth.

But the faces revealed proved to be none other than the two ladies to whose pleadings she had succumbed. Serena fell into Melanie's ready arms in a fit of over-whelming relief, shedding a few unheeded tears.

Cousin Laura's eyes were also moist, she discovered, when she turned to her. But the duenna urged speed.

'You must be gone from here swiftly, before your papa returns. I will lock the door from this side, and Lissett and I will pretend that you have refused either to open it or to answer us.'

'But what will happen in the morning?' Melanie wanted to know, straightening her pink beribboned bonnet as the three ladies went back into the bed-chamber and began a swift selection of suitable garments. 'You cannot pretend for ever that Serena is in her room.'

Cousin Laura drew herself up. 'Tomorrow, I will confess the truth—and say a good deal more besides. I trust that Bernard may be suitably chastened.'

If Serena doubted it, she did not say so. But she trembled for her duenna, and begged her not to court any risk. 'For I have taxed Papa's temper to its limit, and I do not wish his wrath to fall upon you instead, cousin.'

'You do not know your father, child. Even by this time, his temper will have cooled. If he is not already writhing in his conscience, you may call me a simpleton. Believe me, Serena, by the time he has passed a night in the belief that you are cowering in your room in fear of him, he will be a different man.'

Spurred by Cousin Laura to hasten, the two young ladies were soon creeping down the stairs, the butler in the hall below having signalled that all was clear. Clutching a cloak bag containing the most necessary items, and clad in a dark green pelisse with a fur collar, her free hand tucked into a matching muff, Serena bid her duenna a grateful farewell, and hurried out of the house and into the waiting coach.

The Lacey town house was located in Hay Hill, and the drive from Hanover Square did not occupy many minutes. But Melanie nevertheless contrived to extract a brief outline of the day's events from her friend, promising that they should enjoy a comfortable cose when once she had shaken off the inevitable questions of her parent.

'For Mama is bound to wonder why I have invited you to stay with me when you have a perfectly good house of your own. Especially at a time that is supposed to be devoted to the selection of my bride clothes.'

Severely conscious, Serena asked what was to be done. 'Had I better return home again, Mel?'

'Upon no account!' declared Melanie. 'Have you forgot that you are escaping from persecution? Lord, here we are at Berkeley Square already! We shall be at home in a trice. Never fear, Serena. I will concoct a tale that will satisfy Mama, you may be sure.'

Serena did not know Melanie very well, but a week in her company had been enough to reassure her on this point. Besides, she was so grateful for the offered respite that she made no further demur. Though she was far from sanguine about the outcome of Cousin Laura's determination to bring Papa to a more malleable frame of mind.

The carriage drew up outside a pretty establishment, by no means as large as the Reeth house in

Hanover Square, but a perfectly adequate town residence. The ladies descended, and the doors were flung open to welcome the daughter of the house.

Not without some qualms, Serena allowed the footman to take possession of her cloak bag and pelisse—'Take them up with my things, Bordon, and ask Mrs Pawley to make up the room next to mine for my guest' —and followed her rescuer towards a door on the ground floor to the right of the hall.

'For we may as well beard Mama at once,' whispered Melanie as she led the way.

Serena entered behind her hostess into a large drawing-room, done out in a striped paper of pale blue and cream, laced with gold. The theme was repeated in the cushioning to a set of chairs and two wide sofas, upon one of which Lady Lacey was seen to be seated. But no further impression was created upon Serena, for it was to be seen that the lady of the house was not alone.

In a chair by the fire sat the Honourable Mr Camelford, who leaped up to greet his betrothed with becoming enthusiasm. Another gentleman had been standing by a window, so that his profile only was exposed to the door. Serena had taken but a few paces into the room when he turned, and she discovered him to be none other than Wyndham.

Chapter Six

So concentrated had Serena been on her flight from Hanover Square that it had not occurred to her that in this house, the presence of Melanie's cousin was only to be expected. The effect upon her was not one which either duty or common sense dictated. She was overtaken by an overwhelming desire to run across the room and throw herself into Wyndham's arms, pleading for his protection.

It was perhaps fortunate that her attention was captured by Lady Lacey addressing her in greeting. Melanie's mother was a youthful-looking matron, who had retained a good figure and some degree of that warm insouciance that characterised her daughter.

'How charming to see you, Miss Reeth! Have you come to dine with us? Such a pity that you left us the other week. You were sadly missed.'

'Yes, and that is why,' chimed in Melanie, turning swiftly from her betrothed, 'I have invited Serena to stay for a day or two, Mama.'

'To stay? But your bride clothes, my love. Not that I mean to say you are not welcome, Serena, but—'

'Ah, but you see, Mama, Serena is to help me choose. It is so dull to be shopping without a companion! I know you will be with me, Mama, but it will be so much more fun to have my new friend as well.' Sailing across the room again, Melanie put both arms about an extremely embarrassed Serena. 'Now you must not be difficult, Mama, for I positively insist upon having my own way in this.'

'You nearly always do have your own way,' remarked Wyndham, taking a step or two towards Serena and making a slight bow. He spoke with deliberate amiability, as if nothing had occurred to mar the good relations between them.

'How do you do, Miss Reeth? I beg you will not allow Mel's chatter to dismay you. If I know my Aunt Lacey, she will not be so unkind as to turn you out of doors.'

'Heavens, no!' echoed Lady Lacey, laughing. 'Indeed, my dear, I am very happy to have you with us. John, pray ring the bell.'

'If it is for Bordon, Mama, he need not trouble, for I have already arranged everything. Serena is to have the chamber next door to mine.'

Serena found herself herded to a seat beside Lady Lacey, who immediately drew her into the conversation she had been having with her prospective son-in-law before the young ladies had entered the saloon. Serena bore little part in it, for she could not help noticing that the Viscount took his cousin aside where they became engaged in earnest conversation. She could only trust that Melanie would not betray her. To have Wyndham master of the horrible circumstances that had driven her out of her home must sink her into the ground!

'For pity's sake, Mel, what has been happening?' Wyndham was demanding urgently, in a low tone. 'She looks like death! And don't try to fob me off with this taradiddle about your bride clothes. It may do very well for my aunt, but it will not serve for me!'

'Yes, but the thing is,' confided Melanie frankly, 'that I can't tell you. I have not learned much myself. I only know that I found poor Serena hiding in her room in a state of great distress and fear.'

Wyndham felt his chest go hollow. 'Upon what occasion? Has it anything to do with that wretched fellow, Hailcombe?'

'It is no use asking me, George. You had best enquire of Serena herself.'

'How can I possibly do so?' he asked irritably, horribly conscious of that fateful last encounter. 'As things stand between us…'

He was disconcerted to receive a straight look from his cousin, a trifle of unusual seriousness in her face. 'How do they stand, George?'

Wyndham eyed her with suspicion. 'I imagine you must know that very well.'

'I am not in her confidence, if that is what you think.'

'Then you need not look censorious.'

'Do I?' A gurgle of mirth escaped Melanie. 'I wish you will tell Camel so. He can never be brought to believe that I have any notion of censure.'

'I don't wonder!' Wyndham clicked his tongue. 'Keep to the point, Mel. And stop trying to hoax me that you don't know perfectly well what ails Serena.'

Melanie threw up her eyes. 'If you must know, I think it was her papa from whom Serena was hiding. From the little I was able to find out, I believe he is constraining her to marry that dreadful man.'

Not without misgiving, Wyndham noted the mischief that entered her face. 'But if you are bent upon playing knight errant, George, I have a splendid scheme to help you.'

The rose parlour was a cosy room, with pretty pink walls and a neat marbled fireplace, from which a cheerful blaze gave off much needed warmth. It was not merely the bleak imminence of November that chilled Serena. She was haunted by the fear that today Papa would come to fetch her back.

Melanie had averred that she would be safe, here in this little family chamber, to which few guests were ever invited.

'And, in any event, I shall tell Bordon to deny you should your papa arrive.'

With which assurance Serena had to be content. It was dreadful to be scheming against Papa, but what else could she do? Her conscience was sorely troubled, for she seemed to have become caught up in a multitude of prevarications. The excuse that Melanie had concocted for her presence to Lady Lacey had to be overlaid with yet another fabrication.

'It is obvious that you are in no fit state to come out with me, dear Serena. Besides, I am sure you cannot want to be gadding about the shops. I shall tell Mama that you have a headache.'

Since Serena had in fact been dreading the necessity to go out at all—who knew but what she might meet Hailcombe or Papa in the streets?—she was only too happy to agree to this subterfuge. On the other hand, her spirits were too restless for the confines of the little parlour.

She shifted from a chair that gave onto the fire's warmth and went to the window. From there she began to tread a path between the two sets of straight-backed chairs with brocaded seats, which were the only furnishings the parlour afforded, besides a small writing desk and a couple of little tables.

It was all very well to have run away from Hanover Square, but she would have to go back sooner or later. If Cousin Laura failed to turn Papa from his purpose—it could scarcely be otherwise, for her poor duenna could have no influence over him!—what was to be the outcome? But beyond the dread punishment that was meant to bring her to heel, Serena could not think. She knew only that her revulsion towards Hailcombe precluded any possibility of becoming his wife. If Papa proved adamant, she had rather throw herself upon Wyndham's mercy!

Upon which thought, the door opened. Serena happened to be at the window and, turning swiftly, discovered the Viscount himself standing in the aperture.

'Pray don't be angry!' Wyndham said quickly, seeing the startled frown that leaped into her pale features.

'You should not be here!'

He entered the room and closed the door. 'It is most improper, I'm afraid. But there is no help for it, Serena. I cannot stand aside, when I see you looking so white and ill.'

A rush of heat struck at Serena's bosom. Without knowing what she did, she crossed to the nearest chair and grasped its back tightly, as if without its support she must inevitably fall.

Wyndham watched her with a twist at his heart for the further evidence of her distress of mind. Her hair was loose, falling about her face and shoulders, and the figured gown clung, cupping her breasts into tantalising mounds that caused the air to dry in his throat. He dragged his eyes back to her face, and moved to the fireplace, resting one hand upon the mantel.

'What has happened? Or should I first tell you what I suspect?'

Serena shook her head dumbly. Last night she had dreamed of his coming! But the actuality of his presence forced her to confront the impossibility of her misplaced hopes. All the horrid circumstances of their last meeting at Lacey Court flooded back. She had as well court unhappiness in marrying Hailcombe as sue to Wyndham for aid!

'I do not know why you have come here,' she ventured without looking at him, 'nor why you should take it upon yourself to—to—'

'To help you? Have you forgot that I pledged you my word that I would do so?' And then broke it, he might have added. 'Rest assured that I have not come to importune you in any way. I hope you can bring yourself at least to accept my apologies for conduct which was, I admit, unforgivable. I will not repeat it.'

Serena found herself with nothing to say. The remembrance of his passionate caress filled her with warmth—not entirely due to embarrassment. And this last promise left her prey to a stupid disappointment. Without realising it, she took in the strength of muscle outlined by the buckskins and topboots, and found herself fighting against the tug of attraction. Her gaze rose upward, to the smooth-fitting broadcloth coat, the deliberately unruly style of the dark hair. Then she met the grey eyes, and the concern in them quite crushed her.

'Pray do not think of it again,' she said rapidly, as if impelled. 'I assure you I have forgotten it.' May God forgive her for a further lie!

'Thank you.'

It was said in a low tone, accompanied by a diminution of cordiality in his countenance. A frown creased his brow. He gestured to the chair she was holding.

'Won't you sit down?'

Serena complied, folding her hands tightly in her lap and turning her gaze upon the fire, in a bid to diffuse the disturbance of his presence.

Seating himself in the chair opposite, Wyndham let his eyes rove over her features. She was pallid, and shadows hung about the brown eyes. It occurred to him that the eager freshness that had won his interest was conspicuously absent. She was but eighteen, and already the harsh blows of fate had succeeded in damping her spirit. A bitter irony, that the only female who had touched him should have been pushed beyond his reach. But at least he could do what he might in friendship. To leave her to her fate would be intolerable.

'Serena, if you will not confide in me, at least let me give you fair warning.'

The pansy eyes flew up, a startled expression within them. 'Warning! What can you mean?'

Wyndham threw up a hand. 'No threat, I promise you. It is only that I have made it my business to set certain enquiries in train. Forgive me, but I had guessed—when we were at Lacey Court and you told me that you had some quarrel with your father—that the matter concerned Lord Hailcombe.'

A rush of anger spurted out of Serena. 'Mel told you!'

'Not at all. It was my friend Buckworth who had observed you to be often in his company. He had also seen Hailcombe and your father together, and had deduced that he and Miss Geary were encouraging that gentleman.'

'Lord Buckworth has not been the only one to see it!' she blurted out bitterly. 'My cousin says that everyone is daily expecting the announcement of our betrothal.'

Wyndham leaned forward a little. 'Then I most earnestly beg of you to consider well before you engage yourself to a man of whom I have been able to ascertain only the most disquieting of facts.'

It was on the tip of Serena's tongue to refute any intention of engaging herself to Hailcombe, but the words were stayed. With a flicker of something like hope, she recalled that he had earlier spoken of making enquiries.

'You have discovered something to his discredit?'

'And nothing to his credit,' agreed the Viscount grimly. 'Forgive me for asking this, but is your portion of sufficient value to prove a temptation to a needy gentleman?'

'Don't you know?' Serena asked, surprised.

Wyndham emitted a short laugh. 'My offer did not reach the point of enquiring into your circumstances.' He saw the colour creep into her cheeks, and added gently, 'It could be of no interest to me, in any event.'

Because he was himself so wealthy? Or because he no longer cared to marry her? Serena was depressingly aware that her rejection of him might well have caused him to suffer a reversal of feeling. After all, he had said that his shocking conduct would not be repeated. Perhaps he had no wish to repeat it. She dragged her mind back to the point at issue.

'My portion is respectable, but it is not a fortune. Enough to secure a good marriage, Papa has always said.'

And he had seen fit to reject a brilliant one! Which was all at once incomprehensible to Serena. If he was prepared to see her married to a man like Hailcombe, why in the world should he force her to throw away a coronet merely because its wearer led an immoral life?

'Then there must be some other incentive,' Wyndham was saying in a musing tone.

Serena was conscious of a spurt of indignation, and the question was out before she could stop it. 'I presume you mean to imply that he cannot have fallen in love with me?'

'I must be the last man to claim that!'

Her breath caught. Then he did still care for her! Her fingers quivered and she was obliged to clasp her hands tightly together to prevent him from seeing it.

But Wyndham was already regretting his hasty response. It had come perilously close to a declaration. One which he could not make when he knew her father—and Serena herself—to be against him. Pulling himself together, he quickly resumed.

'I am persuaded Hailcombe cannot afford the luxury of a mere attachment. He has no place in the highest circles, as you must know well. It may be that he hopes to improve his acceptance by such an alliance. He is an adventurer, and his career has been a chequered one. That need not condemn him, but you are mistaken if you suppose him to be an honest man.'

'It is Papa who supposes it,' she answered flatly,

out of an unacknowledged disappointment. 'I am led to believe that he is at least respectable.'

'Far from it. I will not distress you with a tale of those exploits of which I have been informed. But you should at least know that he is a man who lives by his wits as well as gaming. Which means, you must know, that he uses dubious methods to gain favours.'

Serena became victim to a curious sensation of *déjà vu*, as if she had heard it all before. Just so had Papa warned her against my lord Wyndham. And now here his lordship was, speaking in much the same fashion against Hailcombe. And with no more explicitness than Papa had used!

Her temper flared, and she jumped up from the chair. 'How am I to know? What are these methods? Are they any more to be deprecated than—than the licentious behaviour to be expected of a—of a libertine?'

Wyndham had risen when she did, but he had stiffened and his voice was ice. 'Is that to my address?'

'Take it as you will!' Serena threw at him, swinging away towards the window, and turning there. 'I must thank you, sir, for your warnings against Lord Hailcombe. It is a pity that you did not think to warn me against yourself!'

'There it is again!' exploded Wyndham, shifting to the centre of the little room to face her. 'What have you been told? Who has dared to throw these slurs upon my name? Of what licentious behaviour am I accused? And what have I done that you should take me for a libertine?'

'You kissed me!' Serena flung at him hotly. 'You used me in a way that—in a way that you might use a—'

'Don't say it!' struck in Wyndham. 'I can guess what you mean, and I have no wish to hear such words upon your lips. But I protest you know nothing of passion, Serena, if that is what you believe!'

'How should I know anything of passion?' she raged. 'I am not a whore!'

With which Serena gasped at her own daring, and fell deathly silent. There was such a blaze of anger in the Viscount's eyes as caused her to quake in her shoes. When he spoke, the deliberate calm in his voice was more alarming than a shout.

'It is as well that you refused me. If we were betrothed, such a remark would certainly tempt me to slap you.'

It had needed only that! Serena crumpled where she stood, half falling to slump upon the window ledge, and covering her face with her hands.

'Go away,' she whimpered. 'It is all of a piece. I had as well submit myself to Papa. You men are bullies all! I do not know why I should have thought you could be any different.'

Wyndham was already cursing himself. What had possessed him to carp at her? As if he would truly dream of offering her the slightest hurt! It was with pain that he saw the fight go out of her. He had meant to bring balm and aid, not push her further into the mire. And what was the implication in her reference to her father? But that could wait.

He came to her and slipped his arm about her where she sagged against the window ledge. She made a feeble effort to push him away, but he ignored it, drawing her forward and guiding her towards the chair in silence. Pulling up the other chair, he placed it close enough that he might take one hand in a comforting hold. Obeying his instinct, he infused command into his tone instead of gentleness.

'Tell me what happened.'

Serena's fingers trembled in his grasp. She was beyond thinking of anything but the deep despair of her situation. The words came haltingly, but she could not withhold them.

'Papa is—is set upon my accepting Hailcombe. He—he does not care that I detest the man. I have b-begged him not to f-force me into this m-marriage, but he is adamant. He threatens to b-beat me into submission, if I will n-not accede.'

She drew a shuddering breath, and Wyndham was obliged to clamp down upon the hot protests that rose to his tongue. Serena was not looking at him, and her free hand plucked aimlessly at the muslin folds of her gown.

'I meant to obey,' she said, suddenly turning the brown eyes upon him. 'After Lacey Court, I made up my mind that I should do so. But when it came to the point—when he...' Her voice faded out, and she shuddered, dragging her fingers free. 'I ran away from him! I hid in my chamber, and Papa banged on the door. I was too frightened even to answer him. Then—then Mel came, and Cousin Laura said I should come away with her.' A huge sigh escaped her. 'But I do not see what is to be done. Papa is bound to come here looking for me.'

'Then he must not find you!' said Wyndham with decision, rising to his feet.

Serena looked up at him, a tattoo starting up in her pulses. 'Why, do you think to hide me?'

He seized her hands and pulled her up. 'No, Serena. I think to marry you! Out of hand, if need be.'

Serena's heart took a leap that deprived her of her senses, and for an instant, the world spun. Had Wyndham not caught her, she knew she must have fallen. But the spurt of joy was swiftly over, and she found herself shaking.

'Pray let me go,' she managed to say. 'Give me a moment, if you please.'

'As many as you like,' replied Wyndham, himself prey to a discomfiting apprehension. He did not release her instantly, for she looked distinctly unsteady, but he relaxed his grip enough for her to slide out. Watching her shift slowly away towards the window, he found himself holding in abeyance a resurgence of the wounding sensations that had attacked him upon first hearing of her rejection.

But this was Serena in person—and the conviction grew upon him that she was going to refuse him, even in this extremity. He fought it down, for at this present he could think of no better method of rescue.

Serena was in turmoil. She was torn between a rash

impulse to give in to him, and an obstinate conviction that if she did so, she would be throwing away all hope of that rosy future she had once dreamed of, envisaging herself as his wife. She turned to look at him, and found his eyes intense with some emotion she did not recognise.

'You are proposing a flight to the border? I am under age. Do you wish for such a scandal?'

'It can't be helped,' said Wyndham brusquely. 'Your situation is desperate, and it calls for desperate measures.'

Overwhelming grief gushed into Serena's bosom, and she turned away. This was not how it should have been! She had never been a languishing miss, cherishing thoughts of romance. A marriage of mutual respect and liking had been all she had hoped to achieve. Nothing had been further from her mind than to discover in herself an obsessive *tendre* for a man to whom she longed to be betrothed.

But the Viscount had drawn her into a fatal attachment, making her foolish with dreams. And now, instead of a marriage that had the approval of all, she was offered a hasty scramble of a wedding that must subject her to the censure of her acquaintance—and the certain disapproval of her parent.

Wyndham moved into the room, driven by more than the desire to extract her from an unhappy fate. 'Serena, why do you hesitate?'

She did not look at him. 'It is not what I want.'

'Nor I, if there were any easier way, but—'

'Pray try to understand!' Serena burst out, moving

to face him. 'Don't think I am ungrateful, Wyndham. It is noble of you to offer it, but—'

'For pity's sake, don't talk such fustian, Serena!'

'—it is a solution,' she rushed on, as if she had not heard him, 'that could never bring contentment. To be forced into it, to take it for an alternative to a worse fate—and the dreadful scandal that must ensue. I could not do it! Nor should you, my lord. It is a recipe for disaster.'

He was frowning now, suspicion in his eyes. 'Not if there is a strong enough bond of attachment.'

The brown gaze met his own boldly. 'There cannot be that—where there is not also mutual trust.'

So she was at that again? Hurt welled up. 'I might have known it! Very well, take your chances with Hailcombe.'

Striding to the door, Wyndham set his fingers around the handle. But without turning it, he looked back.

'One day you will learn how you have misjudged me. I can only hope that you will not too bitterly regret it!'

November, 1811

After a restless night, Friday found the Viscount no nearer an acceptance of his own decision than he had been the day before. Having left Serena, he had put himself through an all too lengthy sojourn at White's, where he had imbibed freely of an excellent claret while animadverting with some degree of acidity on the general recalcitrance and waywardness of the female heart.

Lord Buckworth, who was upon the point of leaving for Brighton, had delayed his departure long enough to advise his friend to go home and put his head in a bucket. Wyndham having bitterly stated his preference for a noose, Buckworth had laughed at him and bid him instead accompany him to the coast.

'No, I thank you,' had growled the Viscount. 'I am in no humour to endure Prinny's excesses. Besides, she need not think that I will leave her to fall like a ripe plum into the hands of that blackguard!'

'Well said!' applauded Buckworth, a teasing glint in his eye. 'I am tempted to remain to pull you out of whatever undoubted scrape you are bound to throw yourself into, but I shall refrain. If a man can't win himself a doting wife without the assistance of his friends, he had better not have one at all!'

Wyndham had toasted this sentiment, tipping the remainder of the contents of his glass down his throat. But with his friend's departure the resurgence of bravado proved brief. If Serena would not marry him in this extreme, she must be wholly set against him. He had as well abandon the game and turn his thoughts otherwhere.

But the obstinate pull of his emotions would not let him. In the long night hours, he kept seeing Serena's face. As she had been in those early days last season, which was in stark contrast to the wan features lately imprinted upon his memory. She might say what she pleased, but she could not deny that she was deeply unhappy. And somewhere in the distant reaches of his mind lurked the conviction that she still cared for him.

It might have been that which sent him riding in the direction of Hay Hill after a vigorous half-hour of early exercise in the Park. Dismounting by the back garden gate, Wyndham called to one of the boys at work within the grounds of the Lacey house, and flicked him a coin to hold his horse. Trading on his close relationship to the family, he then walked up to the house and entered by the conservatory.

About to go through into the hall, he heard Serena's voice close at hand. Checking, he listened for its source, and had just decided that she must be in the room adjacent when he was alerted by the deeper tones of a man. For an instant, he thought it must be Hailcombe, and he strode forward a couple of paces towards an aperture. He knew this connected the conservatory with a summer saloon beyond, where the Laceys generally received visitors in warmer weather in order to enjoy the greenery.

Just as he reached it, he recognised the man's voice to be that of Lord Reeth. Halting before he could be seen, the Viscount unashamedly placed himself in a position outside the opening from which he might eavesdrop. The result was distinctly rewarding, if a trifle wounding to his pride.

To Serena's intense relief, her father's anger appeared to have spent itself. Cousin Laura had done her work well. There was a different air about him, and his manner towards her was a good deal less frightening.

'Laura tells me that you went off with Miss Lacey because you were afraid of me. Is that true, Serena?'

She was sitting in an alcove that gave onto the back gardens, in one of a suite of white-painted ironwork chairs. Together with the potted palms that graced the walls, and a number of exotic plants, the saloon had all the appearance of an indoor garden. It was little used at this season, so Melanie had said, deeming it a sufficiently private spot for this much dreaded visit. The winter sun made it a virtual hothouse, which perhaps contributed to Serena's feeling a trifle overwarm. However that might have been, she could not confront her parent without a degree of trepidation.

'Yes, Papa,' she answered breathlessly, watching him shift with apparent aimlessness in the free spaces of the saloon.

Reeth sighed heavily. 'I am sorry for it. I have been guilty of harshness towards you.' To Serena's mingled astonishment and dismay, he covered his eyes with one hand, and a note of anguish entered his voice. 'My only daughter! It is hard to bear!'

Serena stared at him, unable to think of anything to say. It was such an odd way for him to behave. And what in the world could he mean? What had he to bear? But in a moment or two he had collected himself. Emitting another sigh, he sought for a nearby chair and sat down. When he turned his eyes once more upon her, it struck Serena that he looked older, and careworn.

Impulsively, she leaned forward. 'Papa, are you ill?'

Her father shook his head, seeming to brush off this unaccustomed mood. 'Nothing of the sort. But we must needs be done with this matter, Serena. It is unbecoming in you to fly from your own father's protection. You must come home.'

Fearing to put him out again, Serena checked the protest that rose to her lips. It would not do to point out that she had flown because she needed protecting from him! But she was unable tamely to abide by his wish.

'I beg your pardon, Papa. I was too upset to be thinking of what was right. I want to come home, but I am afraid that you will not listen to my excuses.'

Her father's hands clenched where they were resting on the arms of his chair. 'Your words reproach me!'

'I did not mean it so.'

'I know. You need not explain further. You wish to give me your reasons for rejecting Hailcombe.' His voice became heavy, and he sagged where he sat. 'I would I might accept them, for I know them all. My child, I understand your dislike of the man, believe me!'

A rush of indignation beset Serena. 'But if you understood it, Papa, why—'

He threw up a hand. 'Do not ask me. I cannot tell you. Suffice it that I have a particular reason for this determination. You must wed him, Serena!'

This was utterly incomprehensible. He understood

her dislike, and he was sorry for having driven her to run away. Yet he could not release her from this intolerable future? She was to be given no reason, but she must marry a man she hated? She had as well have eloped with Wyndham after all!

The thought of the Viscount threw her into rapid speech. 'Papa, I have obeyed you in one matter which has caused me no small degree of heartache. Cannot you see your way to relieve me of obeying you in this?'

Reeth frowned. 'You are referring to Wyndham, I take it.'

A crushing at her breast made Serena's voice shake. 'You t-told me that you would have k-kept me at a distance from him had you known earlier of his true character. But it was too late, Papa! And yet I have given him up. You do not know what temptation has been put in my way to disobey you in this.'

'What are you saying?' demanded her father, a slight bark in his voice.

Serena shrank a little, and moderated her tone. 'I only mean to make you realise that I have not lightly disobeyed you in refusing to marry Hailcombe.'

'Yes, but what has occurred between you and Wyndham?'

'Nothing, upon my honour!' Serena assured him, horribly aware of perjuring her soul. Seeing that her parent looked far from satisfied, she sought her mind for some way of deflecting his question. 'I found it difficult to believe that what you told me about him is true. I have tried to ask Melanie—his cousin, you must know—but in a roundabout way. And she has nothing but good to say of Lord Wyndham.'

The Baron snorted. 'Of course she speaks well of him. Do you suppose she would tell you, even if she knew, which I'll wager she does not. No one is likely to have informed a young girl of her years that her cousin was one of the dissolute young men who hung about the Marquis of Sywell and emulated his vicious immorality.'

Despite all her own doubts, Serena experienced a rise of unprecedented fury at hearing the Viscount so described. She curbed it, for any attempt to defend him would inevitably draw Papa's fire. But she could not withhold a little protest.

'Yet it does not appear to be generally known.'

'How do you know? No one would speak of it to you either.'

'Perhaps the tales have been exaggerated,' she cried on a note of desperation.

'Your desire that it should be so, Serena, will not, I fear, make it so,' said Reeth heavily.

A fact of which she was only too well aware. But Wyndham had shown himself again injured by the accusation. If she had not experienced at first hand an instance of his depravity, Serena would have been much inclined to believe him innocent. How little Papa knew her, she realised, not to recognise that it was the very urgency of her desire for the stories to be proved to be without foundation that caused her rather to believe in them.

'Yet have you not seen, Papa, in my willingness to

give up all thought of Lord Wyndham that, despite all tender feeling towards him, I cannot marry a man whose way of life must disgust me? And still you would force me into wedlock with a man whom I can neither like nor respect!'

Her father sprung out of the chair, throwing his hands to his head. 'Heaven defend me, Serena! Cannot you see that I have no choice?'

Serena stared at him, bewildered. 'No choice! No choice but to give me up to such a man?'

Lord Reeth paced for a moment, running fingers through his hair in a way that disarranged the order of his bronze locks. It dawned on Serena that he was distraught. Her heart dropped, and a chill swept through her. Could it be true?

He turned to confront her, and there was a—yes, haunted!—look in his eyes. 'Serena, I regret it almost as much as you do. Perhaps more. It may have been wrong of me not to tell you this before. My child, I cannot save you from this marriage. There is a matter of honour at stake.'

The word struck Serena like a blow in the face. A feeling of deadness crept over her. Honour among gentlemen was sacred. It was the single quality that determined acceptance. To lose honour was worse than loss of life. Everything must fall before it.

She looked at her father, and saw a stranger. With a corroding sense of disillusionment, Serena realised that she was no longer afraid of him.

'I see. You must forgive my ignorance, sir. I had not realised that honour could demand that a man must sacrifice his daughter.'

Chapter Seven

Cousin Laura fidgeted with her spectacles, but it had no effect upon Serena. Disposing herself upon the day-bed in the nursery parlour, she had refused all attempts to dislodge her for any reason whatsoever. She lay back against the cushions she had piled behind her, and fanned herself gently, watching her duenna whip off the spectacles and pace to the door and back again to the fireplace. Then she directed a reproachful look upon her charge, replacing her spectacles for the purpose.

'I suppose you realise that you are in disgrace with your papa, child? I have done my best, but there is no moving him.'

Serena remained unchastened. 'I told you he would not budge.'

'Then I am at a loss to understand why you allowed him to persuade you to come home.'

Serena turned her gaze to the window. 'There was little point in withstanding him on that score.'

Her duenna rustled to the day-bed. 'Yet you persist in refusing to marry Hailcombe!'

'Yes,' agreed Serena, looking round. 'And I will persist despite anything Papa may say or do.'

Cousin Laura sighed, plonking down onto the end of the day-bed. Serena shifted her feet a little, and produced a weary smile. The fan stilled, held so between her fingers.

'It is of no use to try to persuade me, cousin. My mind is made up.'

'And Bernard's no less so!' Leaning forward, she reached for one of her charge's hands. 'I wish you will consider, Serena. Though he exhibits no anger now, I cannot answer for his temper. If it should overtake him again, I am much afraid that he will carry out his earlier threats. You cannot for ever lock yourself in your chamber.'

'I have no intention of locking myself in. Let him beat me if he chooses. I will not yield.'

Cousin Laura's astonished stare would have been amusing if Serena had been capable of laughter. Her duenna let go her hand and sat back, ripping off her spectacles.

'I have never heard you speak so. Are you not afraid?'

Serena's fingers tightened briefly on the fan. 'Of the pain of it? Certainly I am. But I had rather endure that than marriage with that hateful creature!'

'My poor girl, do you not understand? Your father can compel your obedience.'

'By what means, cousin? Unless he intends to disown me and show me the door, I do not see how—'

'He will scarcely proceed to such an extreme,' cut in Cousin Laura. 'But there is nothing to stop him forcing you to the altar. He has even spoken of bringing a priest here to perform the ceremony.'

Serena did not flinch. It was plain that her duenna had no notion how coldly determined she had become. As a means of avoiding Hailcombe, in the last three days she had denied herself when he called, sending a message that she was ill and keeping her room. She had backed this up with written excuses to every hostess to whom she was promised through the following week. And as if that were not enough, she had ordered that all her meals should be sent to her on a tray, either in her room or in this parlour. Cousin Laura came and went, but the only visitor admitted to her presence had been Melanie, who had come yesterday to see how she did.

She had seen nothing of Papa. After their last interview, Serena felt no wish to speak to him. The worth of his regard had been tested, and found wanting. Why should she have any scruple about failing in her duty? She could owe no duty to a father who would throw her life away to save himself. That Papa was conscious of the enormity of his demand had been made abundantly plain, and Serena felt confident that he would not seek her out. The more she took matters into her own hands, the stronger became her will to stand firm. But she had never felt so alone in her life.

'Cousin, it is you who does not understand,' she said patiently, feeling for all her youth as if she were the elder. 'Papa may do his worst, but a marriage ceremony cannot take place without my co-operation. If I refuse to say the vows, I cannot be married. And I will never vow myself to Hailcombe.'

Deep in his cousin's confidence, Wyndham's anxieties had been a trifle laid to rest by the report Melanie had given him. It was Thursday, and November was a week old—a week since Serena had left the Lacey house. His worry had been acute. Much as he applauded Serena's determination—as related to him by Mel—he could not feel sanguine about the outcome. Though her decision to keep her room must afford her protection, the Viscount felt it would prove temporary. From what he had discovered of Hailcombe, he could not but fear that the man would stop at nothing to gain his ends. While as for Reeth—! Here, Wyndham had recourse to a pull at the tankard from which he was refreshing himself in the Long Room at the Castle Tavern.

He had chosen this haunt of the boxing fraternity rather than the austere precincts of White's, in hopes of running into someone who might be acquainted with Hailcombe. All sorts and conditions of men frequented the Daffy Club, and his valet Streatley, who had been set to probe his rival's history, had told him that the fellow was a keen follower of the ring.

But though his eye might probe for someone he knew among those imbibing under the portraits, elegantly framed and glazed, of Mendoza and Belcher, along with others of their ilk who had distinguished themselves with their fists in past battles, Wyndham's mind was elsewhere.

Having been privileged to hear the disclosure that Reeth had made to his daughter, the Viscount had a strong desire to find out just how that gentleman's honour had come to be involved in the matter of Serena's marriage. Passing over the insulting nature of the fellow's remarks upon himself, it had become apparent that his own suit had foundered upon this obstruction.

It was just as he had several times suspected. Reeth had lied when he had said that Serena no longer favoured him. His heart had warmed to the evidence of her regard—culled from her own lips! She had not wanted to believe ill of him. Wyndham knew he had only himself to blame that she had ended by doing so. But the task of proving himself could not be undertaken until all danger to her was past.

The Baron's approval was no longer relevant. The man who could—in Serena's own words!—sacrifice his daughter to his own honour had forfeited any right to a say in her future. Even less could he be permitted to keep her from a man who truly loved her, and who would cherish her to the limit of his own disgrace or death.

But that was for the future. At this present, it behoved him to discover, if he could, what Hailcombe might intend. What incentive drove him, Wyndham could not tell. But if he had failed by fair means to win Serena, would he resort to foul? And what hold had he over her father?

This last was puzzling in the extreme. One would surmise that he owed the fellow money, except that Reeth was no gamester. Besides, the implication of dishonour hinted at something disreputable. Certainly the Baron's political standing could readily be placed in jeopardy.

He was no further forward in trying to think of a scandalous proceeding that might be laid at Reeth's door, when he was hailed by a couple of acquaintances whom he knew from his visits to Bredington.

'I didn't think to see you here, Wyndham,' said one. 'I thought your taste ran rather to swords than fisticuffs.'

Giles Rushford was a man for whom Wyndham had some sympathy. His father having dissipated his inheritance, Rushford was in much the same position as Hailcombe. But Giles was a man of honour, and his position in society was fixed.

Besides, his cousinship to Hugo Perceval, a handsome fellow of excellent family, cast an umbrella of respectability over Giles. For Hugo was nothing if not respectable. The Viscount knew him well, and must admire his uniform prowess at all forms of sport. But he found Hugo too apt to stand upon his dignity. Still, they had enjoyed good hunting together many a time, and he was glad enough to see him.

'How do you do, Perceval? No, Rushford, I am not generally a fan of boxing. I came looking for someone here, that is all.'

'You do not follow the Prince to Brighton?' asked Hugo. 'I had heard that Buckworth has gone there.'

'I have business in town.'

'Then you won't have heard the news?' Giles said thoughtfully.

'Giles, I hardly think—'

'Wyndham is as much our neighbour as anyone, Hugo. He is bound to hear of it sooner or later.'

The Viscount frowned in some degree of puzzlement. 'What are you talking of?'

It was Hugo who answered, his disapproval patent. 'It is only what was to be expected. Yet another scandal emanating from the Abbey. I wish that fellow Sywell might take a fall and break his neck!'

Wyndham began to see daylight. The cousins lived at Abbot Quincey, one of the villages that surrounded the infamous Steepwood Abbey in the vicinity of which Wyndham's own hunting lodge was situated. It was no pleasant thing at this juncture to be reminded of the iniquitous Marquis with whose name Reeth had seen fit to couple his own.

'What has he done now?'

'Driven his poor wife into running away from him,' Giles told him.

'What, the lodgekeeper's daughter he married last year?'

'Bailiff's daughter,' corrected Hugo. 'And it is less than a year since he scandalized the community with that piece of foolishness. The girl was barely one-and-twenty at the time.'

'The more reason for her to run away from the old

lecher,' put in Giles. 'Not but what it is by no means certain that she has run away.'

Hugo Perceval threw his cousin an austere look. 'If you set store by the ridiculous theory that Sywell has murdered her, Giles, I can only say that I do not.'

'Local gossip will have it so, I dare say?' suggested Wyndham, faintly amused.

'Lord, you know what country folk are like! Besides, it hardly accords with that part of the tale which declares there to be gold missing as well.'

'There is that,' Giles conceded. 'The one thing that is certain, Wyndham, is that the girl has disappeared. No one actually knows how long she has been gone, for to tell the truth, very few people have seen her since she married Sywell.'

'Very true,' said Hugo. 'She might have been gone for months for all anyone knew.'

Wyndham was more disgusted by these details when his own integrity had been called in question, than he might have been at any other time. To think that Serena could suppose him capable of the sort of conduct that might drive a young bride from her legitimate home!

'How is it that her disappearance has been discovered, if no one knows when she left the place?' he asked, although his interest in the subject was but tepid. For his part, Sywell was deserving of being abandoned.

'By the usual route, I imagine,' said Hugo, scorn in his voice. 'That fellow Burneck likely told it to the washerwoman.'

'Yes, Aggie Binns is about the only female who will venture near the Abbey these days,' assented Giles. 'As for Solomon Burneck, I have it from my sisters that he has been going about quoting from the Bible again. A habit of his whenever Sywell does anything particularly scandalous.'

The fellow Burneck, an unprepossessing individual with a hooked nose, was valet-cum-general factotum to the Marquis. The Viscount had met him once or twice, and found him a dour character, whose strange loyalty to Sywell had ever been a cause of question. Wyndham felt resentment boil up that Serena should believe him so lacking in taste as to frequent a hell-hole that contained this creature Burneck as well as the Marquis himself.

The cousins continued to speculate, but the Viscount was hardly attending. An unsettling notion had been borne in upon him. How could a girl of Serena's undoubted innocence know anything of that sort of licentious conduct indulged in by Sywell? Even *in extremis*, she had been steadfast in her refusal to marry him. She must have been severely shocked by what she had been told. Had her father or Miss Geary given her some of the gruesome details? Had either of them access to one of the residents around Steepwood? Who there might have chosen to vilify his character?

He was no nearer solving this problem by the time he returned to his lodgings in Ryder Street. He had long since removed from the Lyford family house in Berkeley Square, preferring the informality of this

smaller apartment. It had a severely masculine parlour, containing little beyond a couple of red leather
sofas, and a writing table upon the surface of which
lay the paraphernalia of a bachelor existence.
Magazines, discarded gloves, a dice-box and several
silver containers used as a catch-all for visiting cards,
buttons and other debris. The adjacent bedchamber,
for which Wyndham headed, had only a comfortable
bed, a press and a shaving-stand which serviced the
needs of his toilette. The place was agreeably simple,
in contrast to the cluttered furnishings of his allotted
chamber at home.

Wyndham enjoyed the freedom of it, and nothing
but his marriage would serve to alter the arrangement.
Which brought him to the disagreeable recollection
that at this present his marriage was not in question.

He was greeted by his valet with the depressing
information that Hailcombe continued to haunt the
Reeth house in Hanover Square.

'And in the foulest of moods from all accounts,
m'lord,' reported Streatley, receiving the Viscount's
coat and tenderly smoothing its folds. 'Seems he
don't scruple to show his displeasure, for his man's
been sporting a painted peeper these two days. And
for all he says he had an argy-bargy with a misplaced
door, I take leave to say it was his master's work.'

'You mean Hailcombe gave his own valet a black
eye?' asked Wyndham incredulously, unfastening his
waistcoat.

Streatley laid the folded coat carefully into one of
the drawers of the press. 'If he didn't, there's no call

for Togworth to speak surly of his nibs, which he does, m'lord, make no mistake.'

Wyndham handed him the waistcoat in silence, disquieted by the inevitable reflections that must beset him on discovering that Hailcombe was capable of this sort of petty violence. If the man could lay vengeful hands upon a blameless manservant, what price the safety of a recalcitrant wife? Put in mind of his own foolish threat of slapping Serena, Wyndham's conscience writhed. If he had not done so, would she have flown with him? No, for it had not been that which had stayed her. It was his alleged moral turpitude that had effectively barred him from that form of rescue.

He became aware that his valet was coughing in a meaningful way. He stripped off his shirt.

'What is it, Streatley?'

The valet went to pour hot water from the ewer into the basin. 'There's another matter as might warrant your lordship's attention.'

'Well?'

'Certain company as Togworth has been keeping, m'lord.' Holding a warm towel at the ready, Streatley waited for his master's face to emerge from the basin. 'When I went to meet him at The Feathers, m'lord, he was sitting close and murmuring with a set of fellows as one might expect to meet in a dark alleyway.'

Wyndham lowered the towel. 'Unsavoury?'

'Distinctly so, m'lord.'

A riffle of unease crept into the Viscount's chest. Hailcombe must be hatching something. If his valet was in a string with disreputable characters, the fellow could be up to no good. Had he not suspected as much?

'Keep your eyes peeled and your ears open, Streatley. Try if you can to get the measure of what may be in the wind.'

'I will do my best, m'lord.'

Wyndham passed a fretful night. Early on the following morning he sent a note round to his cousin, asking her to pay a visit to Hanover Square to find out how Serena did. He spent some hours at White's in a bid to prevent himself from brooding. But in the late afternoon, when no reply had been forthcoming, he set out on foot for Hay Hill to find that his cousin had only just returned.

Melanie, fresh as a rose in pink muslin, whisked him into the summer saloon. 'For Mama is bound to want to know the reason if she thinks we are talking secrets.'

'Have you seen Serena?' demanded the Viscount, brushing this aside. 'Is she well? Pray don't tell me that she has given in to Hailcombe, for I know he means mischief!'

'Given in?' echoed Melanie scornfully. 'Of course she has not given in! I told you she was utterly determined, even if her Papa should end by beating her.'

'He won't do that, I am persuaded. But how is she?'

'How do you know he won't? When he has threatened poor Serena I don't know how many times and—'

'Mel, I'll shake you in a minute! How—is—Serena?'

'There is no need to—'

'*Mel!*'

'Dear me, George, you must be in love!' His cousin giggled, as he made a purposeful move in her direction. 'No, don't! She is perfectly well, I assure you. At least—'

'What do you mean, "at least"?'

Melanie threw up her hands, dropping into one of the ironwork chairs. 'Lord, Wyndham, will you let me speak?'

The Viscount took a hasty turn about the room, setting the tassels on his hessians swinging. Then he, too, seated himself, sighing a little. 'Forgive me, Mel. If you knew what I have been through! But never mind that. Only tell me the truth, if you please.'

He was obliged to contain his impatience, for his cousin could not tell her tale without a good deal of embroidering comment. His air of calm was severely tested by an account—which he devoutly trusted Melanie was exaggerating—of Serena's state of mind.

'It seems to me, George, that she is dreadfully unhappy still, despite the strength of mind that compels her to stand out against them all. There is a look in her eyes—I cannot describe it, but—'

'Try, Mel!'

'Well,' pondered Melanie, frowning portentously, 'since you press me, I will say that it was as if the light had gone out of them.'

A shaft of something very like grief struck

Wyndham in the chest. That precious innocence—and it had been destroyed. He would give all he owned to bring it back!

With difficulty, he dragged his attention on to what his cousin was saying, and was conscious of a small degree of relief on learning that Serena was to leave the metropolis on the coming Tuesday.

'Then she will be out of harm's way.'

'Yes, but it is not comfortable for her, poor Serena,' said Mel distressfully. 'She says that her papa is disgusted with her, and that she is being sent home in disgrace.'

'No one is to know that outside of the family,' Wyndham said. 'On Tuesday, you say?'

'The twelfth. Is Tuesday the twelfth?'

Wyndham nodded. 'Four days. Then if she continues to keep her room, I do not see what either Hailcombe or Reeth can do in that time. And it will take her to safety, which is all that matters at this present.'

From this heartening belief he was rudely awakened on Sunday the tenth of November.

Having taken dinner at Limmer's with some of the few friends who had not been lured to Brighton by the presence there of the Prince Regent, Wyndham was enjoying a rare cigarillo, and—at this touchy point in his career—an even rarer moment of conviviality. This was rudely shattered upon receipt of a note from his valet urging his return home at his earliest convenience.

'I know your lordship will wish no delay in receiving the intelligence with which I am regretfully obliged to burden you,' ran this unwelcome missive.

His mind afire with a number of hair-raising possibilities, Wyndham excused himself to his friends and hurried back to his lodgings.

'Out with it!' he demanded of his grim-faced valet, who was waiting in the parlour. 'What have you discovered?'

'Does your lordship recall me speaking of Togworth taking up with some fellows I wouldn't care to run into after dark?'

'The devil! What about them, Streatley? Speak, man!'

The valet relieved him of his greatcoat and hat, and laid both aside, on the back of one of the leather sofas. 'I've been on the watch, so to speak, m'lord, and tonight I saw them again. Togworth wasn't with them at first, so I was able to park myself in a settle just behind so as he wouldn't see me when he did come in. And though they talked quiet, I was able to hear something of what was said.'

Even in his anxiety, Wyndham managed a short laugh. 'Well done, Streatley! I had no idea how excellent a conspirator you could be.'

The valet bowed. 'I am glad to be giving satisfaction, m'lord.' His face became grim again. 'Though I don't see as even the little intelligence I've gleaned is likely to satisfy you in the least.'

With mounting dismay, the Viscount learned that Streatley had gathered an impression of a scheme afoot. But although he could not say where or how, nor precisely what was planned, the Viscount was particularly alarmed by the fact that he was able to confirm mention of a date. The valet Togworth had specified Tuesday the twelfth of November—the very day fixed for Serena's journey to the Reeth estates in Suffolk.

That his visit was unwelcome came as no surprise. Wyndham watched Lord Reeth cross the library to the mantel and grasp it, turning there to confront him.

'If you are come to renew your offer, my lord, I must tell you at once that I have not changed my mind.'

Wyndham's smile was not pleasant. 'Is that why you refused at first to see me?'

He had sent back a message via the butler that he would remain outside the Hanover Square residence until Reeth saw fit to admit him. It had done the trick, as he had known it would. The last thing a politician needed was to arouse speculation in anyone who might chance by to see a prominent member of society parked upon his doorstep.

Reeth's roman nose went up. 'What is it you want, Wyndham?'

'To alert you to the fact that your daughter stands in danger from a set of ruffians whom I believe to be employed by Hailcombe,' said Wyndham without preamble.

A bark of laughter escaped his host. 'Poppycock!'

'Hear me out, sir. These fellows have been heard by my valet to speak of a plot due to be perpetrated tomorrow. Miss Reeth travels to Suffolk tomorrow, I believe.'

'What of it?' scoffed Reeth. 'Was her name mentioned?'

'Not specifically, but the man interviewing these rogues happens to be Hailcombe's valet.'

'And that makes Hailcombe suspect? Your imagination has been playing you false, Wyndham. I say again, poppycock!'

The Viscount regarded him through narrowed eyes. 'Is it? You will scarcely deny that the fellow is a suitor to Serena's hand. Nor that she is resolute in refusing him.'

Reeth's cheeks suffused with colour. 'Not that it is any of your affair, sir, but I deny neither of these facts. I would add, moreover, that you are in no small way to blame for the latter!'

It was Wyndham's turn to laugh. 'I wish it might be found to be so. But I believe Serena to have more commonsense—not to say taste—than to ally herself with such a man. My task, however, is not to bandy words with you on my own account, but to warn you that—'

'Enough!' roared Reeth suddenly, banging his fist upon the mantelpiece. 'I will hear no more of this! If you have barged your way in here to insult my friend—'

'I am amazed that you have the gall to call him friend!'

'*Will you have done, sir?*'

Wyndham checked a violent retort, reminding himself that his purpose would not be served by quarrelling with the man.

'Let us discuss the matter without heat,' he suggested coolly.

'Don't talk to me!' returned the other, rejecting this advice and pacing away from the fireplace. 'Who the devil are you to lord it over me as if you were betrothed to the girl? I refused you, damn it! By what right do you dare to come here?'

'If I had no other right,' Wyndham snapped back, unable to help himself, 'I could throw my honour in your face! Only it is evident that such an argument would scarcely weigh with you, my lord Reeth.'

'How dare you, sir?' raged Reeth, turning on him.

'I am sure you know well enough! Leaving that aside, this alone should suffice. You chose to vilify my character in a way that—'

'Impugning my honour, are you? Not content with insulting my friends, you now choose to insult me, damn your eyes! We'll see, my young buck! We'll see!'

Crossing to the fireplace again, Lord Reeth tugged upon the bell-pull. Turning there, he glared at his visitor, breathing heavily.

Wyndham surveyed him frowningly. This fury was out of all proportion. Was it bluster? Was there a degree of fear beneath the fierceness of those eyes? One thing was certain. Reeth was bent upon giving him no further opportunity to speak his piece. Should he reveal that he knew a good deal more than he ought? No, for that must involve him in admitting to having eavesdropped upon his host's conversation with Serena.

'Before you have me shown out,' he said quickly, for the man's intention was obvious, 'will you at least tell me what merit you see in Hailcombe that you can favour his suit?'

To Wyndham's surprise, a look of revulsion crossed Reeth's features. 'Merit? I wish he had any!'

'Then for pity's sake, what the devil possesses you to foist him upon your daughter?'

The look blanked out, to be replaced with a cold stare. 'I have nothing further to say to you, my lord.'

Wyndham might have argued, but he had heard the door open behind him, and turned to find the butler standing in the aperture.

'Lord Wyndham is leaving,' said Reeth.

Thoroughly disgusted, the Viscount favoured him with a look that he trusted advertised his feelings. 'One last word. I give you fair warning, sir, that I fully intend to frustrate whatever design may have been formed by the person about whom we have been speaking. As for my rights in the matter, I leave that to your own judgement.'

Lord Reeth replied only with a lift of that arrogant nose, addressing himself to the butler. 'Lissett!'

The butler moved into the room, but Wyndham had already turned for the door. His tone became ironic. 'Have no fear! It will not be necessary for you to lay violent hands upon me.'

The man bowed, and passing him, Wyndham withdrew.

* * *

'But why did he come, if it was only to see Papa?' asked Serena distractedly.

'It is no use asking me,' said her duenna, shuffling her spectacles on and off her nose. 'All I know is that he has put Bernard in a towering rage.'

Serena swished back and forth in the narrow confines of the nursery parlour, a prey to confusion. From her station on the day-bed—which had been moved so as to give on to a view of the square below—she had caught sight of the Viscount driving around the far corner. Due to the height of her second-floor window, he had been lost to sight immediately upon reaching their side of Hanover Square. But Serena had leapt up and had her nose to the pane in a moment.

Her heart pattering, she had seen Wyndham stand for some time upon the doorstep, while her mind had run crazily on what it might mean. Since that day when she had repulsed his scheme to save her from Papa's wrath, she had heard of his lordship only through Melanie. His cousin had declared him to be still devoted to her, but Serena had refused to listen. Especially since, along with that affirmation, Melanie had brought tidings of gossip concerning the Marquis of Sywell. A reminder of Wyndham's depravity that could only give her pain.

But today he had come in person, and the disappointment was acute when he failed to request an audience with Serena.

'Could he have gone to Papa to renew his suit?' she suggested, not without a guilty surge of hope.

'Not unless he is a fool,' declared Cousin Laura, seating herself upon the vacated day-bed.

'Why do you say that?' demanded Serena, conscious of an inappropriate annoyance.

'Why, my dear, because he must surely be aware that with all this talk of the Marchioness having run away from Steepwood, your papa is unlikely to have forgotten his involvement with her wretch of a husband.'

Serena halted in her perambulations about the room. She had forgotten that Cousin Laura's friend had also seen fit to burden them with this odious story. It was excessively difficult to stifle an unwarrantable urge to defend the Viscount. Yet she could not keep from speaking her mind.

'You can scarcely lay that at Wyndham's door.'

'Gracious, no,' agreed Cousin Laura, her eyes glinting through the spectacles. 'I am sure Sywell cannot have needed any assistance in driving the poor girl away. Though no one could have blamed her, Lucinda says, if she had gone off with some man.'

'Wyndham perhaps?' suggested Serena scathingly.

'Oh, no, for we would have been bound to hear of it, if that had been the case.'

It could not be, thought Serena resentfully, that the Viscount was too honourable a man to run off with the wife of another!

'Besides,' pursued the elder woman thoughtfully, 'it is not at all certain that Lady Sywell has indeed run away. Lucinda maintains that a number of persons believe that Sywell has murdered her.'

'You don't mean it!' exclaimed Serena, startled.

Cousin Laura nodded emphatically. 'The Roade girls—who live in the same village, you must know— are even said to have spent some time searching for the body.'

Serena shuddered. 'What a horrid place Steepwood must be! I hope I may never go there.'

The spectacles came off. 'There is only one place you are going, my child, and I must say that I am heartily glad of it!'

So indeed was Serena. She had scarcely been able to believe her good fortune when her father had announced that she was to return to Suffolk.

'I own I am astonished that Papa has given up,' she said, coming to sit beside her duenna upon the day-bed. 'I know he has said that he is sending me home in disgrace, but I care nothing for it. I will be out of Hailcombe's reach, and that is all that matters to me.'

Cousin Laura replaced her spectacles, sighing. 'I wish I might believe that our departure signals the end of that man's chances, but I am not sanguine. I think your papa is hopeful that you may come around to his way of thinking.'

'Well, I shan't,' said Serena, not mincing her words. 'I had rather hire myself out as a cookmaid!'

Her duenna was not inclined to give this declaration any credence. 'I fear you know nothing of the life of a servant, child. One week of domestic service, and even Hailcombe would seem a godsend. You had best consider the alternative before you flout Bernard when he next proposes this match to you.'

Serena shrugged. 'Very well, what is the alternative?'

Cousin Laura took off her spectacles, and a sad little smile crossed her mouth. 'I am, Serena. Look at me. Look at my life.'

With which, the duenna rose up and quietly left the room. Serena stared after her, a bleak sense of emptiness pervading her bosom. A despairing protest rose up. That could not be her future! *He* would not leave her to that. He might have gone just now without seeing her—how could he see her, when Papa was so much against him?—but Serena was sure he would marry her in the teeth of them all, if he thought she was to suffer that fate.

Then Serena remembered the Marquis of Sywell, and came down to earth with a bump. Between the devil and the deep blue sea! How in the world was she to decide?

There being no immediate solution forthcoming, Serena sought relief in going to her bedchamber to supervise Mary in the packing of her garments. The task served to distract her mind from the problem of her destiny, and by the time it was finished, Serena was so tired that she dropped readily into bed after consuming the repast brought to her room, and was soon asleep.

The morning brought all the bustle of preparing for departure. When the footmen arrived at her bedchamber to carry her belongings down to the coach, Serena went to her nursery parlour to partake of breakfast. She was writing a hasty note of farewell to Melanie when Cousin Laura burst into the room in a state of unaccustomed dismay.

'Oh, Serena!'

'Why, what is it, cousin? You look as pale as death!'

The duenna's spectacles came rapidly on and off upon each bursting phrase. 'The most dreadful thing—and I do not know what to do! He will not listen to me. I have begged and pleaded—but to no avail. I cannot move him!'

Serena grabbed her arm with one hand, and removed the spectacles from her cousin's wild grasp. 'What in the world is the matter? Tell me, pray. Is it Papa?'

Tears stood in Cousin Laura's frenzied eyes, as she nodded. 'He has had all my trunks removed from the carriage. I think he has run mad!'

'Had all your trunks removed?' echoed Serena blankly. 'But, why, cousin?'

'Because he refuses to allow me to go with you. He says you must travel alone.'

Chapter Eight

Serena fairly gaped. 'But—but you must go with me. How can I possibly travel unchaperoned?'

'Bernard says you will have Mary, and—and that must suffice you. Nothing will move him! I have tried every argument I can think of, Serena.'

'Why? I don't understand, cousin.'

'No more do I. Do you think I have not asked him?' Seizing her spectacles from Serena's slack grasp, she rammed them into her face. 'I declare, I have never been so cross with Bernard! All he will say is that you must be punished, and to go alone will serve his purpose.'

A pulse began to throb in Serena's veins. Why should she be surprised? A father who could prefer his own honour to his daughter's happiness might as easily be as careless of her safety. Not that it was a great distance to the Reeth estates, but she would certainly be travelling all day.

'At least you will not be spending a night on the road,' said Cousin Laura worriedly. 'Although I told

Bernard that an accident might put you to the necessity. What with the weather turning, and the roads so bad, who is to know what might not happen?'

But Serena was too angry to put her mind to probabilities. 'There is always the coachman. I suppose Papa is not minded to let me go without him!'

'Don't be silly, Serena, how could you do so?' chided her duenna, too upset to be susceptible to sarcasm. 'Oh, dear, whoever would have suspected that Bernard could be so careless of your reputation? Setting aside the danger, it is most improper. And you will have to stop to eat. Gracious, you will be alone in a public inn! You must demand a private parlour, Serena, and make sure Mary remains with you. Oh, dear, I only hope you are not seen by anyone who knows you.'

'Well, if I am, it will serve Papa out,' said Serena snappily. 'It is all of a piece. Not that I anticipate any danger, but it just shows how little he cares for me.'

Cousin Laura readily agreed, adding that she had not thought it of him. 'It was bad enough to be forcing you into wedlock—and in so brutal a fashion!—but this goes beyond the line of what may be tolerated.'

Yet there was nothing she could do, as Serena pointedly reminded her. 'Don't fret, cousin. I cannot think that any ill will befall me. Why do you not ask Lissett to make certain to send a groom along with a blunderbuss, if you are so concerned? Papa cannot object to that.'

'He may object if he likes,' said Cousin Laura with

decision, 'but it will be after the event, for I shall not tell him!'

Filled with a new determination, she departed, leaving Serena to her uncomfortable reflections. It was all very well to have buoyed up Cousin Laura with a show of bravado, but the further evidence of Papa's lack of affection could not do other than sink her spirits. No father who truly cared for his daughter could subject her to the indignity and discomfort of travelling for such a distance with only her maid for company. And for a punishment! Was he so lost to all sense of what was due to her? Had his obsession with this arrangement he had made to marry her to Hailcombe completely deprived him of that level of responsibility which she had believed him to possess? And he a politician. What his colleagues might say to such conduct, Serena dared not think.

She had been looking forward to going—not least for the imminent prospect of seeing little Gerald—but now her feet dragged as she went upstairs to fetch her pelisse and tie on her bonnet.

Mary had laid out a thick travelling cloak as well, for the weather had worsened, and the November fogs had started. A weak sun was at present in evidence, but it could hardly be relied upon. And though a hot brick would undoubtedly have been provided, it was bound to be cold in the coach.

Serena had not thought that anything could make her feel worse than she did already. She was in the hall, clad in the furred woollen cloak that covered her shoulders and enveloped the green pelisse, adding extra warmth to just below the knee. The moment had come to say farewell, and she became aware that Lord Reeth was nowhere to be seen.

'Where is my father, Lissett?'

The butler appeared apologetic. 'He is in the book-room, Miss Serena.'

'Does he know that I am about to leave? Shall I go up to him there?'

Lissett coughed delicately. 'His lordship asked me to convey his good wishes for your journey.'

Serena stared hard at the butler, feeling as if a stone were lodging in her chest. 'You mean that he does not wish to see me to say goodbye in person?'

The butler maintained a prudent silence, but the answer was evident in his concerned features.

Serena drew a painful breath. 'I see.'

'Oh, Serena!' wailed the duenna.

If only Cousin Laura had not burst into sobs, and hugged her charge so tightly. If Lissett had not chosen to produce a little flask before handing her up into the coach, urging her to drink.

'A nip will warm you, Miss Serena.'

She obligingly sipped a little of the brandy, and returned the flask, her smile a trifle uncertain. Then Mary must needs weep copiously as she climbed in beside her mistress, clutching a basket of choice sweetmeats sent up by the cook for Serena's refreshment upon the way.

The sympathetic kindness of her well-wishers only served to drive in deeper the hurt inflicted by the one person who ought to have made her comfort his first concern. And Serena saw the waving hands and bravely smiling faces only through a blur as the coach moved off.

Wyndham was only half-aware of the desultory chatter at a slight remove from where he sat. There were few gentlemen gathered thus early in the coffee-room at White's, for it was not yet eleven. And the one he had hoped to see was not among them.

He was deeply troubled, for he found himself at a stand. It was one thing to assert his determination to protect Serena at all costs from Hailcombe's machinations, but when it came to the point, he knew not how to proceed.

He had little enough to go on. He knew that Serena was travelling to Suffolk today, and he had every reason to suppose that Hailcombe intended some mischief. But the rest remained a mystery. It was a great pity that Streatley had not managed to glean anything more useful.

The Viscount had toyed with the notion of confronting Hailcombe with an outright demand to know what he would be at. But the fellow was certain to prove even more obdurate than Reeth. And the devil of it was that, with a ready welcome in Hanover Square, Hailcombe had the advantage of him. He had himself no means of discovering what time Serena and her chaperone meant to set out, although he must guess that they would make an early start. Unless they intended to spend a night on the road, which he could not think to be likely. The journey was lengthy, but in a well-sprung coach, it could certainly be accomplished in one day.

But the coach would make slower progress than his own curricle and four. He felt confident of overtaking it within a very few hours, should it prove expedient to chase after Serena. Indeed, he was rapidly inclining to the view that this would be his best course. In the meanwhile, the presence of Miss Geary must afford Serena protection. But he had already alerted his servants to make certain preparations, and had dropped in at White's in a last-ditch hope that Buckworth might have returned from Brighton, for the Prince, so he had heard, had left there on the ninth, some three days since.

There was no sign of his friend, however, and Wyndham had to abandon a half-formed idea of asking his aid and advice. He uncrossed his legs, which were encased in fashionable yellow pantaloons, and laid down the paper he had taken up. A pretence of reading had enabled him to avoid participation in the prevailing discussion. Just as he did so, he caught the name of his arch-rival on the lips of one of the gentlemen involved, a man by the name of Ingleborough.

'I must say, I never thought that fellow Hailcombe might succeed. Yet I had it from Boulby, who met him last night at the Daffy Club, that he was boasting of his conquest.'

A disbelieving laugh came from one of his companions. 'Her fond father has never consented?'

Wyndham stiffened. There could be no doubt of whom they were speaking. Let one of them but mention her name, and he would know what to do about it!

'I suppose he must have done,' Ingleborough was responding. 'Though I must say, Millhouse, it seems most odd.'

'What's odd?'

'Well, Boulby said Hailcombe claimed that he would have a certain young miss—who shall, of course, be nameless—for his wife within the day.'

'Within the day! What, is it an elopement?'

There was a general laugh, and a sensation of disgust warred in Wyndham with a surge of fury. How dared they bandy her affairs about the club!

'Boulby thinks it's a hum. We all know how arrogant Hailcombe is.'

'Yes, but his quarry is leaving town today,' argued Millhouse, 'or so I heard.'

'If you ask me,' chimed in another voice, whose identity was hidden from the Viscount for his chair backed towards him, 'that golden-haired chit don't like him above half.'

'What's that to say to anything?' returned Millhouse. 'Anyone can see that Reeth is thick as thieves with the fellow. Lay you any money she takes Hailcombe.'

Two of his companions immediately closed with the wager, adding to Wyndham's discomfort. Instinct urged him to call them all to account. But he knew that to do so would serve only to precipitate further talk. He stood up, intending at least to make his presence felt, for he knew well that his own pursuit of Serena was widely known.

Just then the fellow he could not see piped up. 'I wonder what Wyndham will have to say to it?'

There was a flurry of determined coughing from those who were facing Wyndham and had seen him rise. The speaker turned his head, and his eyes popped.

'Wyndham, sir,' said the Viscount in a voice of ice, 'will say that he had always supposed White's to be inhabited by gentlemen—and not by gossiping hens!'

He executed an ironic bow into the embarrassed silence, and walked out of the coffee-room. He was seething, not least at Hailcombe for the possession of a careless and arrogant tongue. Or had it been carelessness? A cold feeling drove through the anger. Had it been part of Hailcombe's scheme to set in train a babble of talk that must inevitably damage Serena's reputation? Was he attempting to make it impossible for her to do other than marry him in order to save her face?

One of the footmen assisted him on with his greatcoat and beaver, and Wyndham, lost in a brown study, almost collided in the doorway with a fellow who was just entering the building. He fell back with a word of apology.

'It makes no matter,' began the other man, and stopped with a look of surprise. 'George Lyford, is it not? Or rather, Viscount Wyndham?'

Wyndham looked more closely, and thought he discerned a vague familiarity in the features of the fellow who was accosting him. He was a man something of Wyndham's own height, but loose-limbed, and perhaps a few years older. He was removing his hat to reveal a head of fair hair, and a pair of grey eyes smiled at Wyndham out of features strongly tanned.

'Lewis Brabant,' said the gentleman encouragingly. 'We used to hunt together some years back. When you stayed at Bredington, remember?'

Wyndham's puzzlement cleared. This was another of the inhabitants of the area around Steepwood Abbey. It crossed the Viscount's mind that the place seemed to have an insistence at the moment on forcing itself upon his notice. Nevertheless, he greeted the newcomer with cordiality.

'You are Admiral Brabant's son. You went to sea, did you not? How do you do?'

Shaking hands, Brabant said that he did very well, but that he had sold out and was in fact just returning home. Dredging his memory, Wyndham recalled that his brother had died a couple of years back.

'Are you leaving? Come back in and have a glass with me,' suggested Brabant.

Wyndham hesitated. While he did not wish to appear discourteous, he was in something of a hurry. Brabant's look became questioning.

'You are pressed for time, perhaps? Don't let me keep you, if that is the case.'

But the Viscount thought he detected a shade of disappointment in his tone, and was conscious of regret. He had warm memories of Lewis Brabant, a less dashing fellow than his brother, but Wyndham had preferred the quieter and more intelligent of the two. Nevertheless, he could hardly afford to delay. His horses were swift, but Serena had all too likely set off already.

He felt obliged to refuse. 'I wish I might, Lewis, but I'm in the devil of a hurry. There's a matter demanding my urgent attention, and—'

Struck by a new thought, Wyndham broke off. Hailcombe had served in His Majesty's naval forces! It might well be that Brabant had known him—or heard of him at least. He might learn something of the man that could be turned to advantage.

Smiling suddenly, he gave his hat up to the footman again. 'But why not, after all? I'll take a glass with you, by all means, Brabant. Though it must be a swift one.'

'As swift as you please,' agreed the other.

Having divested himself again of his greatcoat, Wyndham bade a waiter bring them some wine and led the way into one of the parlours, preferring not to encounter the frozen faces of his earlier companions in the coffee-room.

Several moments were taken up with relating what had happened to various mutual acquaintances, and the discovery that Lewis had advanced to the rank of Captain. Wyndham was searching his mind for a casual way to bring Hailcombe into the conversation, when Lewis disconcerted him by touching on the question of his matrimonial prospects.

'I had heard from some source or other that you were on the point of offering for the prettiest débutante of the season, George. Am I to wish you happy?'

Wyndham fairly winced. 'Sadly, no.'

'I am sorry to hear it, if it was what you wished for. I never heard her name.' He seemed to note the Viscount's unease, for he added quickly, 'But don't mention it, if you would rather not.'

'I have no objection to telling you her name,' said Wyndham, an edge to his voice. 'It is Reeth. Miss Serena Reeth.'

'Reeth?' echoed Lewis. 'She wouldn't be related to the Reeth who is involved in politics?'

Wyndham frowned. 'His daughter. Why, do you know him?'

Brabant shook his head. 'Not him, but his brother. Lieutenant Reeth. We served together on *Neptune* at Trafalgar. Under Captain Fremantle it was then. He was a devil of a fellow, Gerald! Utterly fearless. Too much so, in fact, for it cost him his life.'

'How was that?' It was interesting, if not yet useful.

Lewis related briefly the circumstances of Lieutenant Reeth's death. In the heat of battle, a youthful midshipman had been hit, falling overboard.

'When Gerald saw that he was still alive, he first attempted to throw the boy a rope. But the poor fellow couldn't seem to grasp it. And the sea was aflame below with debris from a burning vessel. But Gerald wouldn't leave him. He stripped off his coat and handed me his sword. Then, before anyone could stop him, he had leaped over the side.'

'The devil he did! Did he succeed in rescuing the boy?'

Brabant nodded. 'No one really knows what happened next. And the boy was too dazed. We pulled him up with the rope strapped about his chest. But Gerald went under—and he didn't come up again. His body was never found.'

It was a shocking tale, distracting the Viscount from his mission as he listened to a recital of the speculation that had attended the death of Lieutenant Reeth. The best guess seemed to be that he had got caught on hidden debris under water, and been burned along with it. The *Neptune* had been obliged to change position in the battle soon after, and no one had therefore been able to determine the precise circumstances.

'He was a good fellow,' Lewis finished. 'He'd have had a Captaincy by now.'

Wyndham made an appropriate response, but he could see nothing in this story to help him. These events had occurred six years ago, and could have no bearing on the present. But it had given him the opening he needed.

'Tell me, Lewis. Did you ever come across a fellow named Hailcombe?'

Captain Brabant happened to be taking a sip of wine just at that moment, and the name appeared to affect him powerfully. He sputtered, choked over the claret and fell into a fit of coughing. Wyndham got up and gave him a buffet on the back. In a moment or two, he had recovered himself, and the Viscount returned to his own chair in frowning question.

'I take it you've heard the name,' he suggested drily.

'Heard it? I've cursed it—and with frequency!'

A rush of triumph engulfed Wyndham, and he reached for the bottle of claret. 'Another glass, my friend? You interest me very much indeed.'

Fifteen minutes later, the Viscount left White's, feeling that his time had been well spent, even if it meant that he would now be further behind in the chase than he could wish. He had occasion, however, to revise this opinion. Awaiting him at his lodgings, he discovered his cousin Melanie, in company with an extremely agitated Miss Laura Geary.

The oppression of spirits that had attacked Serena at the beginning of her journey had lifted a trifle, though it had left her with the sensation of having a dead weight in her chest. Which could not in all honesty be attributed wholly to Papa's unkind conduct. For her obstinate thoughts, refusing to obey her own commands, insisted upon presenting her with a collage of images—all on the same theme. Since there was no point in thinking of Lord Wyndham, it was distressing to discover that she could not get him out of her head. Even more so to find that instead of being thankful to be getting out of London and away from Hailcombe, she was counting the miles that were taking her further and further away from the Viscount. And depressing herself thereby.

For ever since Wyndham's visit to Hanover Square yesterday, Serena realised, she had been foolishly cherishing a hope that his lordship might be proved innocent of the charges laid against him. Had he not said that she was misjudging him? Were it not for Cousin Laura's horrid friend, whose information must be counted impartial, Serena would believe Wyndham. For Papa she could no longer trust.

How dreadful to be obliged to say so! A faint sigh escaped her, drawing her maid's attention. The girl proffered the basket she held, uncovering the napkin in which the various items from Cook had been wrapped.

'Have another sweetmeat, Miss Serena.'

Serena selected a sugared almond, and chewed in silence for a moment, tucking her hands back inside her muff. 'How long have we been upon the road, Mary?'

'Near two hours, Miss Serena. We're just past The Bald-Faced Stag, and will be within the forest in a moment.' The girl apparently felt Serena's tension. 'You've no call to be afraid, Miss Serena. Mr Lissett give orders as Harbottle was to ride on the box with the blunderbuss.'

Epping Forest was certainly one of the danger spots, but Serena knew that there was nothing to fear in the daylight hours. Besides, it was a mere matter of six miles or so to Epping Place, and there were bound to be people abroad.

'I am not afraid, Mary. We are in no danger from highwaymen at this hour.'

Serena saw that her maid was peering at her in the gloomy interior, for the day was dull and heavy with cloud, affording little light to the travellers. The gathering denseness of the encroaching trees as they entered the forest did nothing to improve matters.

'What is it, Mary?'

The maid laid a hand upon her arm. 'I don't like to say nothing, Miss Serena, only you don't seem nowise happier.'

'Don't I? Well, I am finding it a trifle difficult to be happy just now.'

'Oh, Miss Serena, I'm that sorry,' uttered Mary, squeezing her arm. 'But nothing ain't nowise so bad as it can't be cured, you'll see.'

'Will I?' said Serena doubtfully. If so, that cure seemed a long way off.

'I was thinking as how it might be good for you to go home,' pursued the maid. 'I mean, seeing Master Gerald and all. He must miss you something terrible.'

'Thank you, Mary,' Serena said, patting her hand and laying it gently aside. 'I am not unmindful of your care of me. And yes, I am looking forward to seeing Gerald. Only—'

A sudden and deafening report interrupted her, accompanied by a medley of shouts. From without came a confusion of stamping hooves and cursing. The coach lurched, throwing both startled occupants forward. There was a piercing cry, a flurry of hoofbeats, and the vehicle came to a halt.

Serena, her heart in her mouth, righted herself in the seat. Hearing a whimper beside her, she turned to find Mary in a heap on the floor of the coach. A swift decision was dictated by common sense.

'Stay there, Mary!' she ordered in an urgent whisper. 'It will be safer.'

Holding her breath, Serena waited within the dark interior, as shadows passed the window, and a rumble of deep voices indicated the presence of several men. Seconds crawled by while nothing happened. Then the door was wrenched open, and a figure in a mask leaned into the aperture, blocking out the light.

Serena could not forbear a frightened gasp, but she sat still, staring at the monstrous dark shape that observed her in silence for a space. Her heart thumped painfully in her bosom, and all thought was suspended.

Then the figure shifted out of the doorway, and a large gloved hand gestured towards her with a pistol.

'Come on out, missie!'

'Don't, Miss Serena!' quavered Mary from the floor.

'Quiet!'

Let them not realise that there were two females in the coach! Pushing herself up, Serena reached towards the door. She was immediately obliged to grasp at the jamb, for she discovered that her knees were shaking.

Her hesitation caused the masked man to mutter an impatient exclamation. She was roughly seized by the waist, and dragged from the coach. Landing somewhat abruptly, Serena had all to do to keep herself from falling. But in a moment, she had regained her balance, and was able to look about her.

After the gloom of the carriage, there was a surprising amount of light coming through the trees, despite the dullness of the day. The fellow who had ordered her from the coach still stood by its door, surveying her. Upon the box, both groom and coachman were held at pistol point by two masked riders. So much for the precaution of Harbottle and his blunderbuss! The poor man could have had no time to fire it. Another rider, also masked and armed, had reined in at the side of the coach, and was holding a fourth horse, presumably that of her captor.

Serena's glance went from one to the other. All were in frieze coats and slouch hats pulled low over their eyes, lending each a sinister aspect. She felt as if she were trembling all over, and involuntarily clutched her cloak tightly about her. But the only thought in her head was to prevent these undoubted highwaymen from seeing the depth of her fear.

'Is it the one?' came gruffly from the mounted man. 'Can't properly see her face.'

'Nor me,' growled the fellow on the ground. He approached Serena, and she flinched back. 'Now then, me beauty. I ain't going to harm yer. Just want a glimpse of yer hair.'

With which, he reached out and flipped the low-brimmed bonnet, which fell back on to Serena's shoulders, revealing her golden locks.

'Aye, that's she,' confirmed the man on the horse.

'She it is,' agreed his companion, peering closely into Serena's face. 'Yaller hair, brown eyes.'

It was as much as Serena could do to refrain from wrenching away. She was obliged to clench her teeth together, glaring into the fearsome eyes that examined her from above the black handkerchief that hung over the rest of the man's face.

A coarse laugh escaped him as she stood back. 'She ain't short of spunk.'

He shifted away to the other horse and entered into a low-voiced conversation with the rider. Serena breathed more easily, and it occurred to her to wonder why they had not yet demanded any money or jewels. Her mind ran rapidly over the belongings reposing in her trunks, trying to recall which of the more valuable trinkets she had selected to bring with her out of the collection inherited from her mother.

She saw Mary peeking from the open doorway of the coach, and gestured her back with a minute wafture of her fingers. Thankfully, the maid's features disappeared. Serena was only too well aware that while her gentility provided her with some measure of protection—for it was unlikely that these men would do more than take her valuables—her maid's class made her vulnerable. There was no saying what they might not do upon discovering Mary hiding there.

It seemed an age that she waited, while the men conferred together in low tones. Serena had just begun to wonder whether some chance wayfarer might not come to their rescue, when a distant rumble coming from behind signalled the approach of another carriage.

There was a concerted shift from all the highwaymen. Those covering the servants on the box shunted their mounts back a pace. The one on foot took a few hasty steps towards the rear of the coach, and the rider sidled his horse on to the verge.

Serena thought they were poised for flight, and toyed for a moment with the idea of running for the doorway of the coach. But it was obvious that the man afoot was close enough to catch her before she could reach it.

For several moments there was no sound but the growing rumble of the approaching carriage, and the distinct pounding of hooves upon the ground.

Then they ceased, as if the vehicle had come to an abrupt halt. The second rider shifted back to the other mounted men, and handed the rein of the led horse to one of them. Then he broke away. But instead of fleeing, he sped off in the direction from which the sounds had come. Serena had no time to speculate, for the first man took several hasty steps towards her. Instinct made her attempt an escape, but an iron grip caught at her.

'No, you don't! This is where we gets what's coming to us, and I ain't a-losing of it now.'

Her arms were pinioned behind her. A recognition of the oddity of this whole proceeding sprang into her mind. If she had before been frightened, terror now rooted her to the spot. She could not have struggled had she wanted to, for the horridest suspicion dominated her thoughts.

Highwaymen they might be, but these men had a darker purpose. They knew her. They must have been lying in wait for her. She was a prize worth some sort of ransom, and someone would pay them well. And that someone, she felt certain, was in the coach behind.

Sitting bolt upright, her face turned determinedly away from the loathsome creature beside her, Serena strove against an overwhelming desire to scream. With one hand she was grasping the strap, in a grip far stronger than was required by the swaying progress of the hired chaise, which rumbled along behind only one pair of horses. The other hand, tucked under her cloak out of sight—for her muff had been lost in the scuffle—was clenched so tightly that the nails dug into her palms.

She had long abandoned speech. Having vent her outrage in no uncertain terms, she now sat mumchance, refusing to respond to anything her abductor chose to say.

He had not even had the courage to do his dirty work himself. Instead, he'd had ruffians do it for him, exposing her to the roughness of a brutish highwayman.

For upon a signal from his companion who had ridden ahead, the man had dragged her to his horse and flung her across his saddle bow. Serena had heard Mary's shrill protests, which had been summarily stopped—leaving Serena to wonder later what horrid measures had been taken to ensure her silence. She devoutly trusted that they could not have been worse than what had befallen her mistress. Winded, Serena had been jolted for an excessively uncomfortable space—mercifully not far—and had then been dumped unceremoniously to the ground.

Her legs had been trembling, and her breath too short for protest when she saw Hailcombe waiting by the chaise. For several hideous seconds she had remained mute and resistless. But the instant her captor had begun to move, pulling her towards her hateful suitor, Serena had given way to panic. Losing all control, she had struggled madly, shrieking at the unresponsive post-boy for aid until the villain who had her captive had clapped a hand over her mouth.

He had manhandled her into the clutches of the vile beast who now had her at his mercy, and who had not scrupled to show his power. The smart at her cheek had dulled, but she felt battered, and was certain that both her upper arms and wrists would be found to be bruised.

Oddly, the pain of the blow had made Serena more angry than afraid. Her struggles had ceased, but she had poured venom upon Hailcombe's head with words that she had not even known were at the command of her tongue. It was only now, with leisure to recognise the invidious nature of her situation, that the fear had returned. But this time she was determined not to show it.

Outside, the dense trees began to give way to open

country, and it was borne in upon Serena that they were emerging from the forest. With a jolt at her stomach, she discovered that the terrain was unfamiliar, and realised that until this moment she had given no thought to the direction of travel. She remembered that shortly after Hailcombe's chaise had started off, it had passed her own coach and continued upon the same route. But had it then changed direction? Or had she not noticed Epping Place and missed the turn off to Duck Lane at the North Weald turnpike?

Forgetting her resolve not to exchange another word with the wretch who had served her so ill a turn, she turned her head to look at him.

'Where are we?'

Even in the gloom Hailcombe's eyes lowered at her under the heavy brows. A voluminous greatcoat and a hat cocked in the naval style made him appear monstrously large.

'Got your temper back, eh? Trust you've realised that it's dangerous to cross me?'

Serena felt her muscles tighten. 'I said, where are we?'

A coarse laugh came at her. 'You've a deal of courage, I'll give you that. We're past Woolreden, and heading for Waltham Abbey.'

Waltham Abbey? 'Then we are driving cross-country.' A throb began in her chest as an inkling of his purpose seeped into her mind. 'And after Waltham Abbey?'

'Hatfield.' A note of smugness was in his voice.

'On the Great North Road, Serena. I'm sure you know that.'

She did indeed know it. Her stomach lurched. 'Scotland!'

'Bright, aren't you? Yes, we are going to Scotland.'

Serena was so much shocked by this disclosure that she closed her lips upon any further utterance, turning despairing and unseeing eyes first upon the post-boy—heavily bribed, no doubt, since he had been blind and deaf to her sufferings!—and then upon the view beyond the window. It was some time before she was able to control a desire to weep. She would not give Hailcombe the satisfaction of seeing her so reduced.

This resolve was sorely tried as they passed through Waltham Abbey, and when the coach stopped for a change two miles further on at Waltham Cross, Serena even toyed with the idea of leaping out. If she could get away, she might hide herself out in the fields. But it was certain that Hailcombe would catch her before she could reach any sort of haven.

When the carriage turned on to the road to Hatfield, Serena could barely repress a cry of protest. But presently, the pangs of despair gave way to hunger, and she recalled that she'd had nothing but sweetmeats to eat since breakfast.

'What time is it?' she asked, forgetting that she was not speaking to Hailcombe.

Her companion fished out his fob watch and consulted it in the light from the window. 'Going on for two and thirty.'

'No wonder I am hungry! Can we not stop to eat?'

'We'll dine at Welwyn for the change.'

'How far is that?'

'Ten miles from Hatfield, I'd say.'

And for Hatfield, upon enquiry, Serena discovered they had to go another seven or so miles. Oh, it was too bad! Not content with employing those horrid men to drag her to him, he must needs starve her too. She gazed miserably out at the dull day, which only added to her discomfort.

'I'll get you cakes at Hatfield,' Hailcombe offered.

Serena was too sunk in gloom to answer. The time dragged, and her stomach gnawed. When she tried to think how to extricate herself from this intolerable fate, she found her mind as dull as the weather, devoid of ideas.

Hailcombe alighted at Hatfield, and returned with a plate of cakes and a glass of wine. Serena would have liked to spurn them, but her hunger quickened at the sight and she took them gratefully, seizing upon a cake and stuffing it into her mouth. Her escort seemed not to be impatient, but made the post-boy keep the fresh pair waiting for several moments while Serena ate another two cakes and downed the wine.

When they again set off, she felt so much revived that she began to cast about in her mind for some means of escape. But by the time she had discarded at least five promising ideas on the score of their likelihood of casting her into worse trouble, she found herself once again aroused to wrath.

'Why in the world has it to come to this?' she

demanded. 'And pray do not say it is my fault for refusing to marry you.'

'I won't say that,' Hailcombe agreed readily. 'It was your father thought you'd reconsider. I had no such illusion.'

'You cannot mean that you have had this scheme in mind from the outset?' asked Serena, aghast. Had her rebellion been altogether futile?

Hailcombe laughed out. 'What, toil all the way to Scotland? No, m'dear. A forced flight, though, would mean you'd have to marry—or face ruin.'

Serena could not answer him. It had not until now occurred to her that escape could avail her nothing, if once the story came to society's ears. She would be ruined, and would have no choice but to marry the fiend.

But Hailcombe had not completed his disclosures. 'I should have preferred to have married you in a quiet hamlet, somewhere a good deal closer, but your fond father could not bring himself to assist me to a special licence.'

Serena felt sick. 'Are you telling me that Papa connived at this—this—?'

'Elopement,' supplied Hailcombe comfortably.

'Abduction!'

'Reeth won't call it that. He didn't want to know my plans, but I'll warrant he guessed I'd pick Gretna.'

Serena turned quickly away from his mocking gaze, lest the horror she was feeling should be visible in her face. That was why Papa had refused to allow Cousin Laura to accompany her. That had been bad enough. But now to know that he had done it on purpose, so that she might be made captive to a despicable plot—oh, she was lost indeed!

'Why has he done this?' She muttered it half to herself, hardly recognising that she must be overheard. Hailcombe's response almost startled her.

'Why, to oblige me, m'dear. What else? Thought you knew how fondly your father regards me.'

The mockery in his tone was unmistakable. Serena found herself looking round at him again, impelled by an urge to uncover the reason for her sacrifice.

'I know that he regards himself indebted. A matter of honour, he said, but I believe there is more to it than that.'

'Clever of you.'

'Papa must have promised you more than my dowry. Your suit has been too determined for it to be otherwise.'

Hailcombe gave a caustic laugh. 'You're a bright girl, Serena. By my faith, I could value you just for yourself! Come on, then. Tell me what else ''Papa'' offered me—and why?'

'If I knew why,' returned Serena, 'I might have judged of its validity—and spared Papa the humiliation of selling his only daughter for the sake of his honour.'

'And come a willing sacrifice to the altar? I doubt it.'

So also did Serena, but she held her tongue upon the natural retort. Ignoring the taunt, she continued, 'As for what he has offered you, I cannot guess.'

'And you so all-alive! You can't think of the advantage of being the son-in-law of a noted politician and respected member of the *Haut Ton*? You don't foresee that of Reeth's estates, at least one may go to this new member of his family? Young Gerald won't notice a piece missing from his inheritance. Then there's the matter of a regular allowance, which must, from time to time, be enlarged to keep pace with the times. And the expense of keeping Lady Hailcombe in the style to which she is accustomed. And more than that—'

'Pray say no more!' uttered Serena in a stifled tone. She could not bear to hear it. If Papa was prepared to go to these lengths for the security of his honour, the circumstances which demanded it must be dreadful indeed. And this was a man who had spurned Viscount Wyndham on account of his moral excesses!

The thought of his lordship gave her a pang. At this moment, Serena felt she would willingly compound for the man of immoral excesses could she but escape the future mapped out for her by Hailcombe.

The thought had barely crossed her mind when there was a loud protesting shout from the post-boy out in front, and the chaise slowed down and came to a stop. Hailcombe cursed, and opened the hatch to shout at his hireling. Letting down the window, Serena looked out.

Astonishingly, a curricle had been drawn across the road, blocking the way. A groom was at the horse's heads, and a gentleman in a many-caped driving-coat was jumping down into the road. To her intense joy, Serena recognised the features of Wyndham himself.

Chapter Nine

Her heart leaping, Serena fumbled for the doorhandle. How or why Wyndham came to be here were matters which did no more than flit through her head. It seemed to her no less than a miracle, and her only tangible thought was to hurl herself out of the chaise and into his arms.

'No, you don't!' came from behind her, and a strong arm forced her back, holding her hard against the solidity of Hailcombe's person behind her.

'Let me go!'

'Quiet!' he ordered, and with starting eyes, Serena saw that in his hand reposed a silver-mounted pistol, pointed towards the door.

It was wrenched open. Wyndham's countenance appeared in the aperture, fury in his eyes.

'Unhand her, you blackguard!'

Hailcombe's laugh was ugly. 'So easy? Keep back!'

'Wyndham, he has a pistol! Don't you see it?'

Then Serena saw that the Viscount also had a gun

in his hand. But although it should have been trained upon Hailcombe, he was shielded by her own body. Her heart seemed to stop.

Hailcombe's voice mocked. 'My trick, eh?'

To Serena's bewilderment, Wyndham smiled. It was not at all a pleasant smile, but it held a quiet triumph.

'Too previous, Hailcombe. Pray look again.'

Serena blinked uncomprehendingly. But her captor's movement behind her caused her to glance round. In the bustle, neither had noticed that the opposite door had been opened. Through it gleamed the barrel of a musket.

'One move, and my groom will blow your head off,' promised the Viscount. 'Now release Miss Reeth, if you know what's good for you!'

But Hailcombe did nothing. Serena held her breath while he looked first at the musket, and again at Wyndham.

'Think you have me at *point non plus*, eh? And all to be decided upon who fires first.'

'Don't be a fool!' snapped Wyndham, lowering his own weapon a trifle.

'You won't harm Serena, I know that,' observed her captor calmly. 'On the other hand, is your groom going to risk his own neck if I shoot you dead?'

At this point, the groom was heard to mutter words to the effect that he was ready to murder Hailcombe immediately. Wyndham ignored this, and stepped back.

'Since you will have it so, let us agree that at this

present we are even. But that can soon be remedied.'
With an ostentatious gesture, he raised his pistol, uncocked it carefully, and slipped it into his pocket.
'There. Now only come out of that carriage, and I
will fight you for her, fair and square.'

There was a silence. Serena stared in a bemused
way upon her would-be rescuer, hardly able to take
in the rapid turn of events. Hailcombe's voice was
measured, but the mockery held.

'Are you proposing swords or pistols?'

'Swords. I have no wish to make this a killing matter.'

Her captor's mouth crept close to Serena's ear. 'He
thinks me a fool.'

She shivered, and shifted her head, her eyes on
Wyndham's. 'I don't understand you.'

'What, Serena? You don't know how expert with
the foil is my rival to your hand?'

Serena had not known, but her mind fastened upon
that point which most provoked her disgust.
'Wyndham was never your rival! And I will not be
fought over by you!'

The leer was back in his tone. 'I don't think you've
a choice, m'dear.' Then Hailcombe's grip about her
slackened. 'But I do. And the odds are against me.'

Was this defeat? Wyndham knew he had taken a
dangerous gamble in disarming himself. But with
Serena in the way, his weapon was useless. He could
not have risked firing. His reliance was not upon
Hailcombe's honour, for he had none. But unless
Wyndham missed his bet, the villain had a lively

sense of his own safety—and the musket was aimed at his head.

Shifting another pace backwards, Wyndham prepared himself for any trick. If the blackguard would only let Serena come down out of the coach! She was so pale that he hardly dared to look at her, for fear that the sight would distract him. The pistol in Hailcombe's hand was still trained upon him, but the moment the man chose to move he must lose his aim.

Distraction came from an unexpected quarter. The post-boy, until now a pop-eyed spectator of events as he sat the lead horse, chose this moment to object to these unorthodox proceedings. In an eloquent speech, he gave the newcomers to understand that they were no better than the highwaymen who had earlier been involved, and certainly worse than the fellow inside who had hired his chaise, who was a rum touch if ever he had seen one.

'Highwaymen?' echoed Wyndham, his startled eyes flying to Serena's face. Curse the villain if that were true!

'Fine doings on the King's highway!' grumbled the post-boy.

Wyndham turned to him, acid in his tongue. 'There have been worse doings before this. And since you have yourself spoken of highwaymen, I am sure you may usefully be had up as an accessory to kidnapping.'

'T'weren't any of my doing,' said the post-boy, his tone both aggrieved and fearful. He pointed towards the coach. 'He's the one as put them to it, not me!'

'Then if you continue to keep your mouth shut, there will be no harm done.'

'Close as an oyster, yer honour!' said the boy promptly.

Hailcombe snorted his disgust. 'Yes, on my money, curse you!'

Of a sudden, he seized Serena and thrust her bodily from the coach. Too stunned even to shriek, she felt herself falling and knew she could do nothing to save herself.

Wyndham leapt on instinct, catching her as she tumbled through the door. The impact made him stagger and his hat fell off. In the few seconds it took to right them both, he was aware that Hailcombe had acted.

Crouching low, well under the aim of the musket, he had jumped into the road and backed himself against the side of the coach.

Turning with his arms about Serena, the Viscount found himself again facing the man's pistol. Without thought, he put Serena behind him. Where the devil was Bosham with that musket? He met Hailcombe's eyes. The fellow was grinning with an unpleasant show of teeth.

'Thought you'd bested me, eh? Now we'll see who wins!'

Wyndham wasted no words. With an unexpected spring, he closed with the man and, seizing his arm above the wrist, forced the pistol down.

'Let go, you fool, it's cocked!' cried his victim, struggling to withstand the pressure on his arm.

Serena hardly took in what happened. One moment, there were Wyndham and Hailcombe locked in close combat. The next, Hailcombe was sprawling in the road, felled by the butt end of the groom's musket, and Wyndham had possession of his pistol.

'Keep him there, Bosham!'

The groom stood over the inert body, and Wyndham uncocked the pistol and pocketed it along with his own. Then he turned back to Serena.

'Come! He will wake up soon enough, and we must be away.'

She reached out automatically and Wyndham, acting on impulse, pulled her to him, catching her into a convulsive embrace. He had her safe!

She moved a little and the pansy eyes looked up into his. A tremulous smile curved her mouth. 'Thank you!'

Wyndham's heart warmed. 'Did he hurt you?'

'Yes, but no matter for that.'

'Villain!' He released her, and found one of her hands, bringing her fingers to his lips. 'But come now. We will have time enough to discuss it all.'

The next few moments passed like a dream. Serena found herself handed up into the curricle, a rug was tucked securely about her, and soon she was bowling back along the way she had come. She could scarcely believe that her ordeal was at an end. In bemused silence, she looked behind, unable to comprehend that she was not still in Hailcombe's chaise being driven to Gretna Green. She shivered within the woollen cloak, hugging it close about her.

'Are you cold?'

Serena's gaze came back to Wyndham. 'No, I thank you.'

His eyes were on the road. She regarded his profile under the beaver hat, wondering if she were dreaming. Perhaps she would wake up soon, and discover that she had not been rescued. Had it been anyone other than the Viscount, she might not have doubted herself. But that he should have come after her—that he should have known...

'How did you know?'

He turned his head briefly, and the grey eyes were somehow alight. 'Miss Geary went to Melanie, who brought her to me. But I had already a notion that something was in the wind.'

Serena caught her breath. 'Was that why you came to our house yesterday?'

He nodded. 'I could not get your father to listen to me, however. I have had my own valet watching Hailcombe's. The fellow had dealings with the ruffians I take to have kidnapped you. But I had no inkling of that intention.'

'Then how could you have known that you might catch us up on the Great North Road?'

'Logic,' answered Wyndham, with a passing smile. 'It was not difficult to work it out, once I knew you had been sent off alone. I must say that it has been relatively easy to secure your release.'

'Easy!'

'Decidedly.' He laughed. 'I have been driving for no more than two and a half hours, though at a pace that has demanded all my skill, I admit. My own team took me through the first twenty miles, and I was fortunate enough to pick up this one—not of as high a calibre, but they are four good horses. To tell the truth, I had not expected to overtake you before Welwyn, but enquiries at Hatfield rewarded me, and I managed to get ahead of you quite readily.'

'Then you passed us!' marvelled Serena. 'I did not even think to look.'

'Why should you? Unlike me, you had no reason to be studying the occupants of every vehicle.'

'Did you?'

'I had to. But even at the last I was uncertain whether I had calculated aright. The sight of you looking out was decidedly relieving, I can tell you.'

Serena was silent for several moments. It was in an odd tone that she spoke again. 'So Cousin Laura went to Melanie. Because Papa would not let her accompany me, I suppose.'

'I believe she became suspicious of your father's motives,' Wyndham said carefully. 'It seemed to her a bizarre thing to do. She began to think—as I do, Serena—that Hailcombe has some sort of hold over Lord Reeth.'

'I don't know what it is,' she said tensely. 'He would not tell me. Only that he expected to gain an estate and—and money. An allowance that would increase every year, he said.'

Wyndham looked worriedly at her, and discovered that her features were taut. He could readily curse Reeth! Miss Geary had told him—in among the desperate and tearful agitations—how hurt Serena had been by her father's behaviour. If she had now proof of his perfidy, how painful must it be! Let him distract her from that, at all events.

'Do you feel up to telling me just what occurred?'

Serena shivered. 'Hailcombe had four masked men stop the coach. I thought they meant to rob us, but instead they did nothing but wait—except that one pushed off my bonnet to see the colour of my hair. Even then I had no suspicion.' Her voice tightened. 'But when I saw how they reacted to the sound of another coach behind us... I guessed it all then.'

Admiration filled him. 'You seem to have confronted these horrors with a good deal of courage.'

A faint laugh escaped her, and he caught a rueful look in her countenance as he glanced briefly at her. 'On the contrary. When I saw Hailcombe, and that creature made to drag me to him, I erupted into the most cowardly hysterics!'

'But you were far from hysterical when I caught you up,' he pointed out.

Her features became taut again, her tone steely. 'No, for though he used me abominably, I had determined that he should not have the satisfaction of seeing me afraid a second time.'

Wyndham was conscious of a surge of pride. Lord, but she had spirit! Which put him in mind of the tricky task ahead of him. How soon would it be before she abandoned gratitude in favour of war? He had no choice in what he must do, but he doubted if that was going to weigh with Serena.

What complexities awaited him! Was his reward to be just that one glowing look?

The private parlour designated by the landlady for Wyndham's use at the Cross Keys was a small apartment. There was only one casement window and the atmosphere was stuffy, for the fire in the grate smoked a little. There were several chairs set about a square table, which took up the centre of the room, and a couple of wall-sconces gave off so little light as to leave the place in relative darkness.

Wyndham ushered Serena inside, but himself paused upon the threshold, fastidiously surveying the interior. He turned to the woman behind him, about to demand a change. He should have been well enough known at this hostelry not to have been fobbed off with an inferior apartment. But before he could speak, he caught a certain gleam in the landlady's eye, and realised that he had never before baited at St Albans alone with a young lady, and one of obvious gentility.

The recollection that he had laid himself open to this sort of censure could not but annoy him. Yet if a mere landlady presumed him to be upon illegitimate business—and proffered a room suitable to the occasion!—how much more censorious must be the members of his own circle? For Serena's sake, he shut his mouth upon complaint, reflecting that at any rate they would be less likely to encounter anyone they knew in this out of the way parlour.

'Bring some more candles, if you please,' he requested instead, infusing deliberate hauteur into his tone. 'And I should be obliged if you will rustle up some dinner that may be acceptable to the lady.'

Doubt flickered for an instant in the landlady's eyes, and she cast a glance at Serena, who had thrown off her cloak and was standing before the fire, spreading her hands to the blaze. Her voice took on a hint of apology.

'Well, sir, I don't know what you'd call acceptable. But there's pork olives or a raised pigeon pie. Or, if the young lady should happen to fancy it, we've sole as can be baked.'

Serena's head had turned, and Wyndham went into the room towards her. 'This woman has a choice for you, ma'am. Have you any preference?'

Hunger had been gnawing at Serena again for the last several miles of the journey. So much so that she'd been unable either to converse with any degree of ease or to pay much attention to the route. It was past four and thirty, and darkness had already set in by the time they arrived at this place. She had been travelling for some six hours, and she was desperate for food. Yet the thought of eating made her feel nauseous. Or was that because she was so very hungry?

'Nothing heavy,' she said, a shade of anxiety in her voice. 'I don't think I could swallow either pork or fish.'

'Then you shan't try,' soothed Wyndham. He turned again to the landlady. 'Some broth or pottage, if you please, and perhaps a little ham. You may bring the pigeon pie for me.' He smiled blindingly, and saw

with satisfaction that it had a visible effect upon the
stiffness of the landlady. 'Wine, of course, and any
other suitable delicacy, which I leave to your judgement.'

'You may safely do so, sir,' said the woman, thawing considerably. 'Likely the lady is fatigued, and will
find eating a chore. I'm sure we'll find something
she'll fancy.'

She then bobbed a curtsey and withdrew.
Wyndham could not forbear a faint laugh. He went
to Serena, who was struggling with a knot that had
tangled the strings of her bonnet.

'Allow me.'

She stood still. As he wrestled with the knot, her
gaze roved his face, shadowed in the half-light of the
room. It struck her that it was already night, and she
was alone with the Viscount in a private room in a
strange inn at an unknown town. A vein pulsed into
life.

Wyndham worked in silence, acutely aware of the
pansy eyes. A tiny quiver at her throat disturbed her
stillness as his fingers brushed her neck without intent. This was impossible! How the devil was he to
survive the next few days without abandoning every
principle of honour?

The strings came apart, and he sighed out his relief.
He removed the bonnet, and found the golden curls
sadly crushed. Without thinking, he threw the bonnet
aside, uncaring where it went. His fingers shifted to
her hair, and he prinked at the unresponsive locks.

His eyes moved to hers, and found them staring up at him.

His fingers stilled. In the brown depths was a look unfathomable, but one that caught at his heartstrings. He cupped her head between his hands.

'What is it?'

The words were a whisper. Serena responded to its warmth, and spoke the thought in her mind.

'You have taken his place.'

His brows snapped together. 'Hailcombe?'

Serena nodded, with that uncomprehended look yet in her eyes. Wyndham felt accused. Dropping his hands, he stepped smartly back, and turned away from her. Well, it was true! In a way, it was true, he thought savagely.

With hands that shook slightly, he ripped off his driving-coat and, drawing forth one of the chairs, threw it over the back. The beaver hat followed it. Without knowing what he did, Wyndham began to pace the small room, unable to look towards Serena.

She watched him in silence for a moment or two. Why had she said that? It had come from nowhere, as of instinct. But now she did not understand the portent of her own words. She swallowed on a throat grown inexplicably dry, and cast about for her discarded bonnet. Finding it, she placed it on a chair where she had thrown her cloak, and unbuttoned her pelisse. Then she sat down at the table and rested her forehead in her hands, staring down at the white cloth. A suspicion of a headache had begun to nag at her, adding to the nausea that churned along with her hunger.

'I did not mean to compare you to him,' she murmured, half to herself.

'But you consider your situation to be no better!'

The harsh tone sank her spirits. She did not feel equal to answering him. She felt confused, and disorientated. And too ill to enter into this discussion. With an effort, she took her hands from her face and pulled herself upright.

'When do you think we will get to London?'

Wyndham was startled into blurting it out. 'We are not going to London, Serena.'

She looked at him, and he could see the puzzlement, for his eyes had grown accustomed to the poor light. He had thought she had realised that they had turned off the road to London. Perhaps he had misunderstood her earlier words.

'You are not then taking me home?'

'To your father's estates? It would be useless.'

Serena began to feel lightheaded. The conversation seemed to be utterly at cross-purposes. 'No, I meant to Hanover Square. I know we are not upon the road to Suffolk.'

'We are upon the road to Northampton,' he said.

She stared at him. Why was he gripping the chairback in that odd way? Northampton? Bewildered, she put her fingers to her head and rubbed her temples.

'You are tired, Serena.'

'I feel quite sick.'

'Then let us postpone this discussion until you have

eaten. You may not think so, but with some food inside you, you will feel much more the thing.'

His tone had changed again. Serena felt as if she were living in a dream. She watched the Viscount draw out a chair and take a seat to her left. He clasped his fingers together, sighed a little, and rested his chin upon them, staring before him in an abstracted way.

The sensation of unreality persisted. Serena regarded the Viscount with a rising glow at her breast. The months rolled away. In her dreamlike trance, she hardly knew that she spoke aloud.

'When we met, I remember that I said such foolish things to you.' His head turned, and she smiled at him. 'You must have thought me so silly. Only I was silly when you were by. You robbed me of all power of thinking.'

Wyndham did not speak. It hurt him to be reminded of those early days. There was a hush about her as she spoke, a faint echo in her face of that lost innocence that he had so often mourned. And she said it as if it was in the past—as if he were in her past. The suspicion that he had already lost her crept into his heart. Now, when he had her at last, and could not let her go—for her own sake.

'But then you were so kind to me,' she pursued, and her eyes misted. But the smile remained on her lips, and he found it unbearably sweet. 'You were excessively teasing, Wyndham. But you were always kind.'

'Serena—'

He broke off as the door opened behind him.

Turning, he beheld a blaze of light from two candelabra. A waiter brought them in and set them upon the table. Wyndham blinked in the glare, and glancing at Serena, saw her briefly cover her eyes with one hand.

The intimacy was shattered. By the time the meal, brought in by several pairs of hands, had been placed before them, Wyndham saw that Serena's strange mood had given way to growing interest. If he was himself extremely hungry, then Serena must be famished.

There was no further conversation exchanged beyond the strictly necessary for some fifteen minutes, while both took the first edge off their hunger. Serena at length sat back, setting down her spoon and sighing out her satisfaction, for the broth had been wholesome and tasty.

'I find that you were right, sir. I feel much better.'

'You had better eat your fill,' he advised, helping himself to another slice of the pigeon pie. 'We have some way to go yet.'

Which statement effectually killed Serena's appetite, as the unsettling realisation of her uncertain future flooded back. She made no demur when the Viscount served her with several slices of ham and placed the fresh baked rolls within her reach. She ate a little of the ham, but absently. No longer troubled by the confusing state of mind induced by hunger and tiredness, she broached the question without hesitation.

'Why are you not taking me back to London?'

It had come. Wyndham's fork paused halfway to his mouth, and he drew a steadying breath. But it had to be said.

'It would be useless, Serena. Even Miss Geary advised against it. Nor did she suppose it would help matters if I were to take you to Suffolk—though that I did suggest. For I imagine Hailcombe will certainly return to London where he can beard your father. Once they put their heads together, there is no saying what course they might pursue.'

Serena laid down her knife and fork. 'Hailcombe said that Papa did not wish to know his plans.'

'But that did not stop him from making it easy for Hailcombe to have you abducted,' Wyndham pointed out deliberately.

She looked away. After a moment, she put out a hand for her glass and sipped a little of the wine it contained.

'It is no pleasant thing for you to know that your father is in cahoots with that man, Serena, but the fact remains that he is. Your cousin believes that Lord Reeth will continue to assist him.'

What Miss Geary had in fact said to him was, 'It is no good bringing her back here, Lord Wyndham. That man means mischief! He will try again, and you may depend upon it that my cousin Reeth will aid and abet him.'

It had been due to Miss Geary that he had abandoned his first intention of following Serena to Suffolk. He had told her about his warning to Reeth, and she had exclaimed her immediate conviction that there was villainy afoot. A hurried consultation had resulted in his opting for the Great North Road, believing that sooner or later he must find himself either before or after Hailcombe on that route. So indeed it had proved. But in rescuing Serena, he had been obliged to place her in a situation that was even more potentially scandalous.

He had no wish to distress Serena by informing her of the other reason why a return to London was ineligible. What he had heard that morning at White's must have been airing all day through the capital. He could not doubt but that Serena's reputation was already blasted. It was less a case of rescue than one of repair.

'What then do you propose to do with me?'

The question took him unawares. Unprepared, he brought it out flat, with no mitigating preliminaries.

'I am taking you to my hunting-lodge at Bredington.'

Serena awoke in a panelled room that she did not recognise. She was in a plain wooden four-poster, from the corners of which hung curtains of faded yellow brocade which had been left open around her. From a wide sash window to one side, light streamed between the half-open drapes.

She started up on her elbow, and her eyes fell first upon a small press opposite the bed, and a stand upon which were set a basin and ewer. Shifting her gaze, she discovered the gown in which she had travelled, discarded upon a chair near the bed. Instinctively, she looked down at her own person and found that she was wearing a garment that felt strange in feel and size.

Serena threw aside the covers. A man's nightshirt! She stared at the folds of the voluminous garment, unable to imagine how she came to be wearing such a thing. Where was she? What was this place?

A knock at the door startled her, and she dived hastily back under the bedclothes, pulling them up to her chin. The door opened, and the round plump features of a middle-aged woman peeked around it.

'Ah, you're awake, ma'am. His lordship's compliments, and there'll be food awaiting you as soon as ever you're ready. I've brought Joyce here with some fresh hot water, and she'll stay to help you dress.'

His lordship? Serena blinked away the remnant mists of sleep. And then it hit her. *Wyndham!* He had brought her here last night. Bredington. She was at his hunting-lodge at Bredington.

All the evils of her situation came back to her with stunning force, and she fell back upon the pillows with a groan. She was ruined! The man in whom she had foolishly reposed her trust had betrayed her.

'Shall you get up now, miss?'

It was the girl Joyce, bobbing a curtsey and gently peeling away the protective covers. Serena felt herself grow hot with embarrassment. What must she think? Well, it was obvious what she must think. It was what anyone would think, finding her here. The only wonder was that Wyndham had not had the effrontery to have entered the room himself!

Allowing herself to be helped from the bed, Serena blushed again at the shocking nature of her attire. But it did not apparently trouble the maid, who was pouring hot water into the basin. Why should it affect her? Serena cannot have been the only female to have been found in so compromising a situation in this dreadful place.

The events of the previous night began to piece together in her mind as she dealt automatically with the business of preparing herself for the day. It was soon clear why she had been dressed in a man's nightshirt—was it Wyndham's? She had no clothes with her other than those she had been wearing when Hailcombe's bullies had taken her from her own chaise. She wondered how he had proposed to clothe her for the few days it would have taken to reach to Gretna Green and back again.

But that was scarcely relevant. For the Viscount, who had rescued her from a hideous marriage, had instead brought her to the very establishment that had been the hotbed of his horrid lusts. True, he had said that there was no other course open to him. But Serena had refused to be persuaded of this. The moment he had mentioned Bredington, she had been unable to withstand a violent wave of hideous suspicion.

She had been hushed and anxious for the rest of the way—near three hours in an open carriage which had left her well nigh exhausted. Indeed, she thought she must have fallen asleep towards the end, for she had little memory of their arrival here. And none of being put to bed. A dreadful thought assailed her.

'Who undressed me last night?' she asked abruptly of the maid.

The girl was doing up the buttons of her gown, but she paused in her work. 'It were me and Mrs Pitchcott, miss, his lordship having carried you in. We tried to wake you, but you was that tired. His lordship says as how you'd been on the road for ten hours or more.'

There was shocked awe in Joyce's tone, but Serena's attention had caught upon the intelligence that she had been borne into the place in Wyndham's arms. A betraying pulse pattered for a minute or two. She suppressed it, and put another question.

'What time is it, if you please?'

'Past noon, miss. His lordship said as how you weren't to be disturbed.'

His lordship said! With a little spurt of rage, Serena wondered just what else his lordship may have said. What reason had he given for his scandalous arrival with a genteel female in his company? Or were these people too used to such doings even to be concerned at the impropriety of it?

By the time she had donned her only gown, the green kerseymere in which she had chosen to travel, and was ready to follow the maid through a lengthy passageway and down some stairs, Serena was in a state of nervous expectancy that caused flurries of butterflies to leap about her insides. She came down into a modest hall, with rooms going off in several directions. The whole place appeared to be panelled, including the parlour into which she was ushered.

Serena hardly noticed much beyond the dining-table set with a white cloth, and the hunting scene of a painting on the wall ahead. For Wyndham sprang up from a seat at the end of the table, and executed a small bow of welcome.

'Good morning—or rather, good afternoon.' His voice sounded stiff, his manner overly formal. 'I trust you slept well. Won't you take a seat?'

After one brief glance, Serena refused to meet his eyes. She made a business of taking the seat to one side which the maid Joyce pulled out for her, and allowed herself to be wholly distracted by the offerings emanating from the woman she recognised from earlier and who introduced herself as Mrs Pitchcott, the housekeeper.

There was coffee, and griddle cakes, with a selection of jams and cheeses to be spread upon them. 'Or if you prefer, ma'am, there's potted asparagus and pickled mushrooms.' With which Serena was offered slices from a fresh brown loaf and good country butter.

She chose at random, unable to think beyond the Viscount's pervasive presence at the end of the table. To her consternation, once she had been served and the coffee-pot left within reach, Mrs Pitchcott withdrew. Serena looked round at the closed door, feeling her stomach go hollow. Unable to help herself, she cast a flying glance at Wyndham's face.

'Have no fear,' he said drily. 'You are in no immediate danger. It is not my practice to seduce young

ladies when they are attempting to eat their first meal
of the day.'

Her cheeks hot, Serena dropped her gaze to her
plate, staring unseeingly at its contents. She took refuge in her coffee-cup, sipping at the hot liquid.

'That is what you think, is it not?' demanded
Wyndham after a moment. 'Perhaps I should rather
have continued on to Gretna with you.'

Serena put down her cup. A quick breath gave her
courage to look at him. 'Why didn't you?'

Wyndham hesitated. She'd had someone catch her
hair up into a topknot and the change was distracting.
She looked childishly young. The thought crossed his
mind that green became her delightfully. Mentally he
kicked himself. She had asked a question, and was
awaiting his answer.

He wanted to say that he had chosen this way in
hopes of repairing the damage, and mitigating the
scandal. To have gone to Scotland could only have
resulted in worsening it. He had already put his plans
in hand, for his groom had taken his curricle to
London with a letter for the Baron. But since he could
be by no means certain that Reeth would obey the
summons—even less that he could be induced to
bring Miss Geary to play propriety—he was loath to
tell Serena what he had done. He was certain that
Hailcombe would try to retrieve Serena, and it was
all too probable that Reeth would help him. It was
evident that Serena's father was resigned to the scandal, if Wyndham was not.

'I had no wish to marry you in such a scrambling way,' he said, prevaricating.

'You had no objection before,' Serena pointed out flatly.

'The circumstances were different.'

'How?'

Again he found himself hovering over his answer. It occurred to him to wonder why he was shielding her. She must know the truth sooner or later. To withhold it was serving only to increase her suspicion of him. Yet it went against the grain with him to distress her further. Had she not borne enough? He temporised.

'If I had married you out of hand then, Serena, all that would have been said of it was that we had taken the step only because your father would not consent to our marriage.'

'Whereas on this occasion?' She looked him boldly in the eye. 'What is it that they might say now, if you please?'

He might have known her intelligence was of too high an order to be fobbed off. Fortifying himself first with a few sips of the ale with which he had been refreshing himself, Wyndham capitulated.

'Serena, you do not understand the workings of Hailcombe's mind. He had prepared things well.'

Serena frowned. 'You mean because he hired those men to fetch me to him so that he could not be blamed?'

'I am not talking of the highwaymen he hired. It is what he saw fit to put about before he went. Even in my hearing, the matter was already being speculated upon. By the time I got to you, I dare say the story he told was all over town.'

Her countenance paled, and Wyndham at once regretted having begun upon this. If he knew Serena, she would not be content with innuendo. Nor was he mistaken.

'What s-story?'

The tremor in her voice racked him, but there was no going back now. 'That Hailcombe would have you to wife within the day. What would anyone suppose, knowing you were going out of town, but that a flight to the border was intended?'

To his dismay, Serena's brown eyes grew dark with rage. Her voice shook. 'And what will they s-suppose, do you think, when I don't come back m-married? When they hear from Hailcombe that I am now with you?'

He reached out as if he would take her hand, but Serena snatched it away. Wyndham drew back, hurt. Stiffly, he answered this.

'I am persuaded Hailcombe will say nothing so prejudicial to his interests. If he shows his face, people will only think that you are at home in Suffolk.'

'Then why should I not have gone there?'

'And laid yourself open to your father's schemes?'

Balked, Serena turned away. Without realising what she did, she took another sip of coffee, thinking furiously the while. He could have taken her back to London! Why should people say anything bad of her if she returned there? She might have made up some tale to account for it. The coach had been found to require attention, perhaps. Or her maid had been taken ill. Anything.

But in London, she remembered, she would be as much at the mercy of Papa's complicity in Hailcombe's machinations as if she had gone to Suffolk. She looked again at Wyndham.

'Very well, but why did you bring me *here*?'

'Because it is the safest place I can think of.'

'Safe?'

He flinched at the scorn in her voice. 'I am aware that you believe it to be a haunt of vice, but the fact remains that it is secluded enough for a hiding-place. No one need know that you are here.'

Serena eyed him, challenge in her face. 'And now that I am here, what do you propose to do with me?'

A somewhat unnerving smile curved his mouth. 'Why, marry you, Serena. What else?'

Chapter Ten

Serena jumped so violently that she almost upset the coffee pot. 'But how càn you marry me? Unless you have procured a special licence, you cannot marry me anywhere but Scotland. You know that I am under age.'

'Which is one of the reasons why I could not take you to my mother at Lyford Manor—even though she approved of you.'

She eyed him with acute suspicion. 'What other reasons had you?'

Wyndham threw up his eyes. 'For pity's sake, I should have thought that must be obvious!'

'Not to me.'

'What do you suppose my father's reaction would be,' he demanded brutally, 'if I arrived at Derbyshire—in a curricle, if you please, and with a débutante at my side!—announcing that I had intercepted her flight to the border with another man, and that I intended now to marry her myself?'

A flush rose to Serena's cheeks, and she glared at

him. 'Why do you not add that she was already living under your protection, for it is no less than the truth?'

Wyndham was tempted to tear his hair. 'Cannot you see, you little fool, that my sole desire is to brush through this with the minimum of scandal?'

'I see that you are trying to hoax me!' she retorted. 'You have already said that you had no wish to take me to Gretna Green—'

'It is not that I did not wish for it, but—'

'—and if your intentions are truly so honourable, why should you bring me to the very place where you are wont to bring those sort of women who—'

'Serena, that is the most complete—'

But Serena was on her feet, her temper flaring. 'Don't dare to tell me that I have misjudged you! I tried to give you the benefit of every doubt, my lord Wyndham. I almost argued myself into believing that it was Papa who had fabricated the whole, in order to put me against you. But now I see that it wasn't so, for—'

'*Will* you allow me to speak?'

She halted in mid-stride, her breath catching. The Viscount had risen too, and for an instant she stared at the blazing grey eyes in defiance. But the sheer fury in his voice cut straight at her heart. Dropping into her chair, Serena dumped her elbows on the table, and covered her face.

Wyndham's anger dropped right out. Sighing, he resumed his seat and reached out for the flagon of ale. As he emerged, he saw that Serena had resumed her meal, making a praiseworthy effort to behave as if nothing had happened. But her hands shook as she attempted to butter a slice of bread, and he was hard put to it to refrain from reaching out to her again. She would only flinch away!

'I beg your pardon,' he said quietly. 'You have been through a great deal, and the last thing I want is to quarrel with you, Serena.'

'No,' she agreed dully. 'Not if you wish to persuade me to become your mistress.'

Wyndham felt his temper rising again, and repressed it. 'What must I do to convince you? Why do you persist in this ridiculous delusion?'

She looked at him. 'I would not if it had been only Papa's notion. Before Hailcombe came into our lives, he had been happy enough to consider you for my prospective husband. He told me himself that until he had learned of your association with the Marquis of Sywell—'

'My *what*?'

'It is of no use to look like that, my lord,' said Serena rebelliously. 'Do you suppose I would still believe that you were one of the men he has corrupted if I had not heard it from another source?'

'Corrupted!' Wyndham's eyes narrowed dangerously. 'What other source, pray?'

'Someone who lives here. Miss Lucinda Beattie.' She brought out the name with a defiant lift of her chin. It was a name she had come to dislike amazingly, but she was not going to tell that to the Viscount.

He was frowning. 'I have never heard of her.'

'She is a friend of Cousin Laura's, and she lives in—in Abbot something, I think it is called.'

'Abbot Giles?'

'Very likely.'

'Not that it matters.' Wyndham eyed her balefully. 'So it is upon the evidence of some gossiping tabby that you choose to condemn me.'

'I don't choose to!'

'Of course not,' he agreed, with awful irony. 'You are forced to, because I have brought you to Bredington. Even though anyone with the least bit of common sense must perfectly understand my reasons.'

He rose from the table and threw down his napkin. 'Very well, Miss Reeth. Believe what you like. I have done!'

With which, he stalked from the room, slamming the door behind him with unnecessary force.

The early-morning mist made it extremely difficult to see, and the cold penetrated without mercy through the pelisse. It had not been designed for walking in an unknown forest in the middle of winter. Serena was glad she had been wearing kerseymere underneath, and not muslin, when she was captured. How had she come to forget her woollen cloak?

She was beginning to regret that she had taken this step. Only now that she was fairly into these dreadful woodlands, she doubted her ability to find her way back to the hunting lodge. She had lost sight of the river, by which means she might have trailed a route back to the point where she had forded it, close to Bredington itself. It must have been a regular crossing place, for the stones were numerous and flat, and the bed of the river visible below the clear waters.

But it was useless to think of it, for she was certainly lost. She was weary to her bones as well, having tossed and wept into her pillows for the better part of the night. What else was she to do after such a horrid day?

Wyndham had disappeared after their quarrel—ridden out, the housekeeper said. Serena had spent a miserable day, cooped up in the front parlour. She had been obliged to acknowledge the masculinity of the place with its leather-bound chairs, a chest in one corner, upon which reposed a discarded whip, several old copies of *The Gentleman's Magazine*, and a pewter tankard. On a table nearby were a number of decks of cards, and the pictures on the walls had been all of sporting subjects. There were no signs of female invasion—not that it proved anything!

The Viscount had returned only at five. By which time Serena was feeling so furious and lonely that she had announced her intention of taking dinner in her room.

Had his lordship demurred? No, he had not! Instead, he had bowed in a manner that was wholly dismissive, not to say rudely ironic. Serena had flounced off in a temper. Not that she had eaten much of the meal that had been brought to her on a tray. What she had managed to swallow might as well have been ashes, and she had wasted far too much time in listening for a footstep in the corridor beyond, in the vain hope that a tap at the door might bring Wyndham—penitent and ready to use every art to persuade her to believe in him.

But Wyndham had not come, and Serena had been wretched. The miserable counsel of the night had brought only one desire—to escape from Bredington. Which had led her to this undoubted folly.

The eerie silence of the forest was broken by the snapping of a twig. Gasping with fright, Serena froze, shrinking back against a tree and peering about her into the shrouding mist.

An indistinct shadow moved ahead of her. No, two shadows. Serena's heart began to thump with fright. They were coming this way! As stealthily as she could, she crept around the other side of the tree trunk, which was large enough for concealment. A murmur of voices approached.

'D'you get anythin'?'

'Nowt but a brace o' hares.'

'One for the pot, eh?'

'Sparse pickings. But there's winter for yer.'

Serena held her breath, not daring to peep as the men passed close. Their progress was so silent, she could almost have sworn that no one was there. But another twig or two snapping confirmed they were now on the far side.

Creeping quietly round the tree, she dared to look, and saw again only shadows. They might never have been! She set off in the opposite direction, with only one thought in her head. To get out of this horrid forest.

A couple of hundred yards further on, she saw that the mist ahead was thinning a trifle. Through it, beyond the trees, there was empty space. Lifting her skirts, she hurried, and presently came out into open country, sighing with relief.

Halting, she looked about, for the mist was clearly lifting. To one side she saw a lone cottage of a fair size, and headed towards it, intending to ask for refuge, or directions at least.

A dour-looking maid opened the door. She was of middle years and sturdy build, and her brows rose at sight of the visitor. She looked Serena up and down.

'And what might you be wanting, may I ask? Trifle early to be paying morning calls, ain't it?'

Serena was daunted. She had not thought how odd her sudden appearance must look. But before she could think how to answer, an interruption occurred. From behind the maid's broad figure could be glimpsed a screen that did not quite conceal the room beyond. A brisk voice was heard.

'Do shut that door, Janet. You are letting in the cold!'

'You'd best come in,' said the woman to Serena, and stood back to allow her to enter. Then she shut the front door and led her directly into a sizeable room that looked to be a parlour, which had been pressed into service for other purposes. An open stairway was to be seen on the far side, and a dining-table was placed by the window. The room was bright from a cheerful fire in the grate, and upon a sofa placed to catch its warmth sat a young woman with a child upon her knee. She noticed Serena with evident surprise.

'Why, what is this?'

'No use asking me,' said Janet. 'Found her on the doorstep.'

And with an air of washing her hands of the whole affair, she vanished through a door at the back, leaving Serena to make her explanation.

'I beg your pardon, ma'am, but I came from Bredington, and lost my way in the forest. I wanted to ask if you...'

Her voice petered out, for the expression had changed in the face of the young female whose house she had invaded. It was a face sharply intelligent, with eyes of an attractive green—just now showing puzzlement, or perhaps doubt? Her hair was drawn back, and partially covered with a frivolous lacy cap which tied under the chin. It was dark, in stark contrast to the abundant curling locks of the child, which were of a shining red-gold, and which the woman had clearly been in the act of brushing.

'Bredington?'

There was more than question in the one word. Serena felt herself blushing, and blurted a protest. 'Oh, I know what you must think! But it is nothing like that. At least, it was not meant to be. Only I have run away from him, and—and I don't know what I should do!'

A pair of dark brows were raised. 'Him? Is it Lord Buckworth perhaps?'

'Oh, no. I scarcely know Buckworth. It is Wyndham.'

'Viscount Wyndham? But why in the world—' She broke off, and suddenly smiled. 'Forgive me, my manners are atrocious.' Setting the little girl down, she rose and held out her hand. 'How do you do? My name is Annabel Lett, and this is my daughter Rebecca. Becky, say hello to the lady.'

But the toddler, who was clinging to her mother's skirts and staring up at the newcomer out of two wide blue eyes, only buried her face in the folds of Annabel's petticoats.

'She is shy with strangers.'

Serena smiled, said that it did not matter and introduced herself. A bustle followed, while Annabel went through to the kitchen, where she said the maid had gone, demanding tea. She was a woman of quick motions, with a trim figure and a decisive manner. When she took Serena's pelisse and hat and discovered how chill she was, she pushed her into the sofa to be warmed by the fire.

In a short space of time, Serena not only found herself partaking of tea and toast, but so compelling was the personality of Mrs Lett—a widow, as she explained to Serena—that she found herself pouring out her trials. The men in the forest, so Annabel surmised, must have been poachers.

'The villagers—in particular the tenants of Steepwood—are known to poach the forests in winter.

Sywell is so mean a landlord that one feels they have some excuse. They are not dangerous, however, and I feel sure they would not have harmed you, even had they seen you.'

The mention of the Marquis recalled the worst of Serena's troubles to her mind, and she could not withhold her upset. It was a relief to talk, especially to a female who neither exclaimed like Melanie nor scolded like Cousin Laura, as Serena related how she came to be staying at Bredington.

'You poor girl!' was Annabel's comment at the end of this agitated recital.

She had resumed her task of brushing her daughter's hair, but had given the little girl up to her maid after that redoubtable dame had brought in the tea, and the two ladies were now alone. To Serena's surprise Annabel, who was seated in a chair opposite, took her hand and held it.

'You have had a dreadful time of it, but I do think you ought to consider well before you throw away this promising solution.'

'You mean of marrying Wyndham? But I don't know that he truly means to marry me.'

'He said so, I think you told me.'

'Yes, but I don't believe him!' stated Serena defiantly. 'In any event, would you marry a man who is an intimate of the Marquis of Sywell?'

Annabel stared at her. 'Who told you so?'

'My father—whom I do not believe. Only my cousin had it from Miss Lucinda Beattie, who is her dearest friend.'

Her hand was released, and Mrs Lett sat back. 'I see. Well, I do not wish to say anything unkind of Miss Beattie. She is a worthy woman, and I have every reason to like her. But there is no denying that she lives for gossip. I cannot approve it, for gossip can be so extremely hurtful.'

She drummed her fingers on the chair arm, and Serena thought a faintly wistful expression had crept into the green eyes. But then Annabel seemed to brush it off.

'But the poor thing has little enough else to entertain her, and people around here are only too ready to condemn. One cannot blame her if she adds up two and two to make five.'

A faint hope stirred Serena's bosom. 'Are you saying that it is not true?'

Annabel smiled. 'All I will say is that I have lived here some two years, and I have never heard any ill of Lord Wyndham. Buckworth is a known rake, but even his name has not been coupled with that of Sywell. The Marquis, you must know, is an exceptionally vicious specimen. I should be astonished if the likes of the lords Wyndham and Buckworth, so far from following him, did not utterly condemn his activities.'

Serena's spirits were lifting, but still she was not satisfied. 'But were there not women of ill-repute staying at Bredington last summer?'

A little gurgle of laughter escaped Annabel. 'To my knowledge, you are the only female to come out of

Bredington. And you, it would seem, are betrothed to its owner. I see no room there for gossip.'

Wyndham had passed perhaps the wretchedest night of his life. He was forced to realise that he had supposed, in a nebulous way, that once he had Serena safe the rest would take care of itself. So much for that! Had he been so foolishly confident of her regard? Though there had been a moment, in the inn at St Alban's, when she had shown him a degree of affection.

The devil fly away with the girl, for she *did* care for him! Only she had fastened upon this ridiculous notion about his supposed association with Sywell— of all people. A man whom he had viewed with the utmost disgust from the first. Indeed there was not one of his acquaintance hereabouts who had a good word to say about the Marquis.

Well, he had Reeth to blame for it, as for everything else. His valet hovered with starched replacements while he tied his neckcloth, thinking unkind thoughts of Serena's father. In fact, where was the fellow? He had half expected him to arrive late last night.

Even as the question formed in his mind, a knock at his bedchamber door brought Pitchcott, the lodge-keeper, with a message from his wife to say that Lord Reeth had arrived, and was awaiting the Viscount in the front parlour. A surge of expectation threw Wyndham's pulse into high gear. Now they would see! Five minutes later, clad in buckskins and a blue frock-coat, he walked into the front parlour, ready for battle.

Reeth was standing by the window, looking out, the burnished head a trifle sunken in shoulders that stooped. He had not troubled to remove his greatcoat, though it hung open to reveal a wine-coloured coat beneath. Wyndham took in the change in him as the man turned. He looked haggard, his features grey, and there was strain in the eyes that searched Wyndham's face. He looked as if he had lost flesh, and if the Roman nose stood out as prominently, its arrogance was gone.

Shocked out of his antagonism, Wyndham regarded him blankly. Why had he not noticed this deterioration in Serena's father at their last meeting? Perhaps he had been too much involved in his own anxiety.

'Have you married her?' demanded Reeth harshly, but with less than his usual bark.

'Not as yet.'

'Damn your eyes!' muttered the other. 'Why not?'

Astonished at the question, Wyndham frowned. 'How could I, without a special licence? Or your permission, if it comes to that.'

Reeth seemed to sag where he stood. 'Why in Hades did you not take her to Gretna Green?'

Wyndham moved into the room. 'My object, sir, is to avoid scandal, not create it. I wrote as much to you.'

'A waste of time. We are all doomed to scandal now.'

Puzzled, Wyndham watched him cross the room

and drop into one of the heavy leather chairs, throwing up a hand to brush at his hair in a weary gesture. What ailed the fellow?

'Forgive me, sir, but I am afraid I do not understand you. When last we spoke—'

'Don't remind me!' He rubbed heavily at his forehead. 'You don't know what it cost me to—' He broke off, and looked up at Wyndham. 'But it gave me hope! If you could be induced to act—which you did!—and his plans went awry, that damned bloodsucker could not set it at my door.'

For a moment the Viscount did not take it in. The enormity of the implication was almost more than he could believe. Rage boiled up inside him.

'Do you mean to tell me, my lord Reeth, that you deliberately put your daughter through a terrifying experience in order that I should be induced to rescue her?'

Reeth glanced up at him, saying with something of his usual bark, 'It is not as bad as that. I had no hand in the arrangements. I merely tried to make it obvious that there was devilry afoot. And without rousing that fiend's suspicions.' He sighed, and a note of self-loathing entered his voice. 'I have been reduced to skulking in my house, that he might not find me, with my butler primed to say I was from home. I came with your groom in the curricle, starting out in the early hours.'

'Which is why, I presume, you have not brought Miss Geary,' suggested the Viscount.

'I couldn't. Hailcombe was bound to come looking

for me, and if we were both absent, he would smell
a rat. Though he left a letter at my house, I imagine
even now he believes me to be ignorant of what tran-
spired. Lord knows I wanted to be!'

'But you were not, sir,' Wyndham pointed out ac-
idly. 'Otherwise you would not have sent Serena out
alone.'

He received a fierce glare. 'Do you think it was
easy? Do you know what it has done to me to be
obliged to behave to my only daughter in so savage
a fashion?'

'Not only your daughter,' Wyndham said through
his teeth.

The Roman nose was directed at him with some of
its old arrogance. 'Yes, I attacked your character. I
had to. It was easy enough. I knew Sywell of old, and
you had this hunting-lodge convenient to the Abbey.'

'So you forced Serena to believe there was a connection—and painted a lurid picture that gave her a
disgust of me!'

Reeth sunk into himself again, sighing. 'I didn't
have to. Laura has an acquaintance here. Another old
maid. I knew I could rely upon their propensity for
gossip and exaggeration. Between them, they succeeded in putting Serena off.'

'You are mistaken.' Wyndham shifted to the window, and looked out. 'Even now she is fighting
against her inclination. But her heart is constant.' He
turned. 'Despite your best efforts, my lord Reeth!'

The elder man flinched slightly. 'My hand was

forced. You don't know, Wyndham, what a blow was promised me if I did not acquiesce.'

'No, I don't know,' Wyndham said, deliberately cold. 'I wish you will enlighten me. What hold has Hailcombe over you?'

Reeth sagged deeper into the chair, and his hands covered his face in a gesture so like to Serena's that the Viscount almost felt sorry for the man. After a moment, the hands dropped. The Baron looked more ill than ever. It was evident that he had suffered. But that, thought Wyndham, hardening, did not excuse his conduct.

'You may as well know it. The world will know it soon enough, for I have made up my mind to let him do his worst. I will not help him further.'

And not a moment too soon! 'Well, and what is his worst?'

Reeth's head drooped. 'The matter concerns my brother. He was a naval lieutenant.'

Wyndham jumped. 'Lieutenant Reeth? He was killed at Trafalgar, I believe, and died a hero.'

A fleeting glance was cast up at him. 'So the world believes. So I believed. The truth is otherwise. He jumped ship rather than face the enemy.' Disgust and pain throbbed in Reeth's voice. 'A deserter! Gerald Reeth—a man for whose passing I grieved so deeply that my own wife's death was lessened in comparison.'

'This is what Hailcombe told you, I presume?'

Wyndham held down the elation that was growing in him. He was by no means eager to put Lord Reeth out of his misery. Let the man suffer a few moments longer.

'He also served on *Neptune*. Hailcombe saw Gerald go over the side.'

'And you believed him implicitly?'

Reeth snorted. 'Do you take me for a fool? Of course I didn't believe him. At first, that is. I have contacts in the Naval Office. I made exhaustive enquiries. But you don't know these war records. They deal in essentials, they have to. The individual is sacrificed to the cause. ''Missing in action.'' That is all they could show me. Oh, I had the usual letter at the time. Anyone who dies in battle is presumed a hero.'

A faint cynical smile crossed his face. Wyndham was conscious of a curious enjoyment in prolonging the man's agony. But it would not do.

'Many who die in battle are indeed heroes,' he began.

He was treated to another explosive snort. 'Yes, but not Gerald Reeth! You perceive the trend? I could find no evidence to refute Hailcombe. I could not allow him to besmirch Gerald's memory. The talk, the scandal, the disgrace—it was not to be borne! Dishonour is a blot that stains for ever. True or not, many people would believe him. Besides, Hailcombe claims to have seen Gerald two years ago, in a foreign port.'

'He lied!' Wyndham crossed to the fireplace and faced Reeth, who was so lost in his tale that he had barely looked up. 'Hailcombe lied, sir. Believe me, the whole story was nothing but a fabrication.'

'Much you know! Why should you say such a thing?'

Wyndham could not forbear a smile. 'I might not have done so a few days since. Only it happens that I most fortuitously met an old friend of mine on the very day Serena left London. He is Captain Lewis Brabant, and he was also on *Neptune*.'

He had Reeth's full attention now. The man sat up. 'He was at Trafalgar?'

'He was, and knew your brother well. He spoke of him highly, and told a very different tale. In fact, if I am not much mistaken, he is likely in this area at this moment, for he lives near Steep Abbot not two miles from here.'

The Baron rose eagerly from his chair. 'Good God, man, do you say so indeed? Is it possible that he may be the means for me to confound Hailcombe?'

'He had ammunition aplenty, sir. One tithe of the articles upon which he indicted Hailcombe would serve you! The man is unprincipled beyond belief.'

'Take me to this friend of yours, I beg of you!'

'I had rather bring him here to you, for—'

Wyndham broke off, as a knock at the door interrupted them. His housekeeper entered, looking a trifle harassed.

'What is the matter, Mrs Pitchcott?'

'It's the lady, my lord!' said the woman in distress. 'I went to see if she was awake, and she wasn't in her room.'

Wyndham's heart stopped. 'Have you looked for her?'

'Joyce and I have searched the house from top to bottom, my lord. She's nowhere to be found.'

It was purely by chance that he saw her. Frantic with anxiety, the Viscount had been on horseback within minutes of hearing that Serena was missing from Bredington. He had cursed his way out of the house, ignoring his valet's shouts regarding his great-coat and hat. His first instinct had been to follow the track that led to Steep Abbot, and he had started out in a bang, riding hell for leather.

His mind had been rather on the previous day's quarrel than a common-sense approach to finding her, and he had expended much energy in cursing himself for allowing the estrangement to have been prolonged. Serena had run away from him with nothing but the clothes on her back. Anything might have happened to her. God send her steps had not taken her anywhere near Steepwood Abbey!

But Wyndham had gone only a few hundred yards when his native good sense had reasserted itself and he had reined in. She could not have been out of the house before daylight, and she must anticipate that he would search for her. It was unlikely then that she had headed down the only road out of Bredington. Which had left what? The forest of Steep Wood lay all about his hunting-lodge. Serena could not have meant to lose herself. If he had himself fled in like fashion, Wyndham reckoned that he must have chosen at least to navigate by following the river that ran alongside the lodge.

Turning his horse, he had backtracked, crossing at the ford, for he had calculated that Serena would have wished to put distance between herself and the lodge. His way had led him down the River Steep until he emerged from the trees and rode towards the foot-bridge that carried a pathway up via the village of Steep Ride. Surely Serena must have followed that route? What must he do? Call at every cottage, if need be.

Only a small doubt had assailed him. Had she been in a frame of mind to think logically? Could it be that she had sought a path through the forest and become lost? She might even now be lying somewhere in among the thickset trees, injured and undiscovered.

The thought had sent Wyndham hurtling up the open turf, heading back towards the forest, which he had skirted, riding a little inside it, within the trees. His eye had been trained upon the dark interior, a growing dread sending him unpalatable images of disaster. That he had turned his head just as he was passing the fateful cottage, Wyndham ever afterwards counted as instinct. For there was Serena!

Her hat was off, her pelisse unbuttoned, and she was chasing an infant around a fenced off area of garden. Even as he saw her, she caught the child, who let out a shriek of delight. Wyndham saw the toddler lifted in Serena's arms, and the sound of her laughter floated to him over the intervening space. His heart contracted, and he turned his horse towards the cottage to which the garden obviously belonged.

Breaking into a canter the instant he was clear of

the trees, Wyndham saw that Serena caught the sound. She stood still, the infant held in her arms, watching his approach in silence.

Her thoughts were suspended, and the only thing she was conscious of was the thudding of her heartbeat in her chest. Then she felt Becky being drawn out of her arms, and found Annabel beside her. She was smiling.

'I believe he has come for you.'

Serena could not speak. The Viscount was already dismounting, looking for a convenient rung on the fence where he might tether his horse. It seemed only moments before he found the gate, and presented himself in Annabel's garden.

Serena's heart was still beating like a ticking clock. What was she to say to him? How to get over the dreadful awkwardness that must attend any attempt at speech? Was he furious with her for running away?

She ventured a peep at him as Annabel introduced herself. Wyndham did not look to be irate, though his eyes were fixed on her face. Serena instantly dropped her own gaze, feeling her cheeks grow hot.

Wyndham was far from angry. He was instead conscious of a dreadful hollow feeling at his chest. She could not even look at him! Had he ruined all with his—yes, petulance!—that had resulted in her choosing to run away rather than marry him? His eye caught the female hovering to one side. She had given him her name, but he could not recall it.

'I must thank you for your kindness to my—to Serena,' he said, just stopping himself from speaking of her in intimate terms to which she might object. He wished fervently that the woman might go away!

Mrs Lett appeared to read his thought. 'I will leave you, sir.' But she did not immediately go. 'Serena!'

Serena jumped, turning quickly. 'Yes, Annabel?'

Her new friend leaned close, but her words were audible to the Viscount. 'I am persuaded that you would do well to listen to anything his lordship may have to say to you.'

With which, she settled her daughter upon her hip, and quietly re-entered the cottage. Serena was left confronting his lordship in the deserted garden. Her chest thumped unbearably and her tongue cleaved to the roof of her mouth.

Wyndham eyed her, hesitating. She was at least waiting, but her gaze shifted this way and that. How should he begin?

'Why did you run away?'

She glanced at him only briefly, but the look in her eyes reproached him. No, that had been the wrong thing to say!

'I didn't mean to ask that. I know why.'

The pansy eyes shifted again, and met his. 'Do you?'

He drew a breath. 'Because we quarrelled. Because you believe me to be a confirmed libertine. Because—' He broke off and raised helpless hands, shrugging eloquently. 'No, I don't know. I don't even know what to say to you, Serena.'

Reflecting that she was as much tongue-tied,

Serena gathered herself together. 'It was a silly thing to do.'

'Extremely silly. Lord knows what danger you might have run into!'

'I knew you were angry with me!'

He put out a hand. 'I am not, I promise you. Only you did give me a fright.'

A fleeting smile escaped her. 'Not as big a one as I gave myself. I was lucky to have happened upon Annabel.'

She was thawing, he decided. A surge of hope went through him. He took a risk. 'Serena, would you have come back?'

The blood flittered down her veins. He ought rather to ask if she could have stayed away! But before she had an opportunity to reply, Wyndham spoke again.

'No, don't answer that! What I meant to have said is—*will* you come back?' His voice dropped. 'With me.'

She wanted to say yes. She wanted to throw herself upon his chest, crying out the misery she had long been suffering on his account. Yet some instinct of her sex prevented her. A need of which she was only vaguely aware.

Her hesitation was torture to Wyndham. The devil! Did she yet question his integrity? Well, there was a new element now, he remembered. Reeth must vindicate him!

'Your father has arrived.'

Startled by the abrupt announcement, Serena stared at him blankly. 'My father?'

'He is at Bredington.'

'At Bredington!' She eyed him in something of a puzzle, feeling dazed. 'How did he know?'

Wyndham's smile was wry. 'I wrote to him yesterday—before you awakened.'

'You never told me that!'

'You never gave me a chance!'

She bit her lip, a hint of resentment in the brown orbs. Wyndham quickly flung up a hand. 'Don't let us quarrel again! I should have told you, only there was so much else to say. And to be truthful, Serena, I could not be sure he would come.'

'Indeed, no,' agreed Serena wonderingly. A horrid thought assailed her, and she paled. 'He has not brought Hailcombe?'

'By no means,' the Viscount reassured her. 'In fact, he was bent upon foxing Hailcombe—which is why he ignored my request for him to bring Miss Geary.'

In a few brief words, he put Serena abreast of the latest development, laying far more credit to Lord Reeth than he believed the man deserved. It had made Serena desperately unhappy to be at outs with Reeth, and he had no wish to widen the distance between father and daughter.

Serena listened with a resurgence of the flutter in her veins. He had not meant to hoax her! His intentions truly had been honourable. Oh, she had misjudged him terribly! She wanted desperately to tell him so, but that instinctive caution prevented her. The sense of something missing grew.

She discovered that as they talked they had turned

together without intent, walking further down the garden, a little away from the cottage.

'Is Papa then amenable to a match between us?' she asked without thinking, and then flushed as she recalled the unsatisfactory nature of their present relationship. She tried to retract, and faltered hopelessly. 'I mean—is he not...does he say that—'

Wyndham turned, catching at her shoulders. 'Serena, it is not your father's agreement that troubles me! If he could stomach Hailcombe—even to save your uncle's name—he is unlikely to balk at me, whatever he believes.'

'But has he retracted what he said of you?' asked Serena anxiously.

The Viscount let her go and dropped back a pace, wounded despite himself. 'Can you bring yourself to trust me only upon Reeth's word? Serena, this is a man, be he never so much your father, who has shown himself to be susceptible to blackmail! Must he serve as witness to my good character? Why can you have no trust in me? In my deeds, if nothing else!'

The disquieting need flowered, and all at once Serena knew just why she had run away. He might have commanded her trust at any time, had he only told her the one thing she yearned to hear! Only he had never said it. Not even yesterday, when he was trying to persuade her that he indeed meant marriage. Was she to presume it? No, my lord Wyndham, it would not do!

'Why did you rescue me? Why have you persisted all this time when you knew how I distrusted you?

You could have left me to my fate, Wyndham. I rejected you. I spurned your aid when you offered it. And you would wed me still. I don't understand. Tell me why!'

Wyndham stared at her blankly. 'Do you mean to tell me that you do not know?'

'If I knew, I would not ask you!' she retorted, snapping.

A short laugh escaped him. 'Then you are either foolish beyond belief, or more innocent that I had supposed! I love you, simpleton. Does that answer you?'

Serena's heart thumped, and her voice shook. 'It is you who is the s-simpleton! You n-never told me so b-before. If you had, I should never have b-believed those w-wicked lies I was told about you. If I did, it is your own f-fault!'

Light broke over Wyndham's countenance, and the warmth crept into his eyes. 'Serena, you unprincipled wretch! How dare you say so?' He seized her by the shoulders once again, and shook her. 'What you mean is that I am already vindicated. Who told you the truth? That woman who took you in?'

A rueful smile lit the pansy eyes. 'Annabel, yes. She said she had never heard anything bad of you, and that Miss Beattie is a dreadful gossip.'

'Exactly so.' He eyed her with mock severity. 'I don't know what you deserve, Miss Reeth!'

'For misjudging you? I cannot be blamed for that.'

Wyndham drew her closer. 'That I concede. But to

pretend that you didn't know my feelings for you, when—'

'But I didn't!' Serena protested. 'Oh, I hoped— *desperately*. Only it did not seem possible that you could truly love me.'

'Oh? What then do you suppose made me persist in trying to win back your regard, my darling little idiot?'

A shy smile crept into the brown eyes. 'Well, that was what led me to hope, you see.'

His lips twitched. 'Did it indeed? Yet when you had the opportunity to secure my affections for ever, you ran away!'

'Because you abandoned all attempts to persuade me of your honourable intentions. What else was I to do?'

Wyndham could not forbear a spurt of laughter, but he caught her into his arms. 'Your logic defeats me, my adorable innocent. But this you may depend upon. If you again mistake my caresses for those of a libertine, I shall know what to do about it!'

Serena smiled shyly up at him, and the tattoo was again at work in her veins—in pleasurable anticipation. A mixture of mischief and innocence entered the pansy eyes, reminding Wyndham irresistibly—and poignantly!—of those early days of their acquaintance.

'You will first have to give me an opportunity to make such a mistake,' she pointed out.

Which provoked the Viscount into offering her an instant opportunity that left her breathless and trembling. No hint of dismay overtook her as she became engulfed in the heat of his passion. Instead the satisfying thought flitted through her mind that the future must offer him every chance to repeat the experiment.

She opened her eyes to find his burning glance devouring her face. 'Oh, George!' she breathed, involuntarily using his given name.

'Yes, my sweet?' he murmured, nuzzling her cheek.

Serena gave a little shiver of delight, and sighed. 'Once again, if you please, for I am not perfectly sure if—'

She was not permitted to finish the sentence, and this second assault upon her senses was undertaken in a manner that left Serena so weak at the knees that Wyndham was obliged to cradle her for fear that she might fall.

He gazed down into the lovely countenance, a glow in his chest for the dreamy look that had settled upon it, and the long-sought return of pleasure in her eyes. He twined one of the gold locks around his finger.

'Now do you see why I moved heaven and earth to win you?'

She gave a deeply satisfied sigh, and smiled at him. 'Yes, and I am so glad.'

'Which means, I trust,' said Wyndham, a glint entering his eye, 'that my sentiments are reciprocated. If I did not speak of my feelings, you have certainly been reticent about yours. But I happen to know that you love me. Pray don't attempt to deny it, for I may as well confess that I heard you say so to your father.'

'When?' Serena demanded, abruptly pushing him away, her cheeks flying colour. 'I am sure I never said I cared for you within your hearing.'

He grinned, catching her back into his embrace. 'You did not know it, but I overheard you speaking with him in the summer saloon in Melanie's house.'

'Eavesdropping! Wyndham, how could you?'

'I have no compunction,' he returned. 'For I would not otherwise have known enough to be suspicious of your father's motives in acceding to Hailcombe's demands.'

Serena was outraged. 'That, yes. But you were not to know then how much I loved you.'

'And now?'

'You deserve that I should refute it!' Then she relented, sinking against him, and sliding her arms about his neck. 'Oh, George, I did care for you so much. And the worst of it was that the more I tried not to, the more entangled I became.'

'Don't I know it!' agreed the Viscount feelingly. He kissed her again, his lips lingering over hers. His voice became husky with passion. 'I am glad I had all to do to win you. I might not otherwise have recognised how very deeply in love with you I am, Serena.'

Such a gratifying sentiment could not go unrewarded, and it was some time before either had leisure for the exchange of any further words. But presently Wyndham roused himself sufficiently to suggest that they should repair to Bredington to set her father's mind at rest.

Farewells and thanks had to be said to Annabel Lett, and then the Viscount took Serena up before him on his horse, settling her in the crook of his arm. She gripped his coat with one hand, and the pommel with the other, the ribbons of her bonnet precariously clasped in her fingers.

The way was beguiled with the laying of plans. Wyndham proposed to travel to London within the day, both to obtain a special licence and bring Cousin Laura back with him—together with some much-needed garments for his betrothed. Their wedding should be celebrated in the shortest possible order—Serena breaking in to suggest that Mrs Lett should be invited to witness their nuptials—and thereafter they would travel first to Lyford Manor to break the news to his parents.

'And after?'

'There is bound to be a deal of talk, and I would spare you that,' said Wyndham, kissing the top of her head, which was resting just inside his shoulder. 'Would you care to go to Italy for a spell? And Greece perhaps?'

Serena leaned snugly into him. 'Anywhere you wish.'

Wyndham's tone became teasing. 'This is novel, Miss Reeth. Have I so suddenly become the undisputed arbiter of your movements? I had no notion I was gaining so even-tempered a wife.'

A giggle escaped Serena. 'Well, but it is not as if I had any other destination to offer.'

'If you had, I presume I might count myself lucky to have any say at all in where we went.'

'No, how can you think me so contrary?'

He drew rein, but only so that he might clasp her within the circle of his arm. 'If I have learned anything from these past hideous weeks, it is that behind the sweet innocent that originally won my heart lies a woman of courage and spirit. And,' he added tenderly, the smile warm in his grey eyes, 'I adore her in every guise.'

As his lips gave her proof of this utterance, Serena felt the last little doubts melt away. She had blamed him for not speaking of his feelings before, but in this she discovered she had erred. She ought rather to be thankful. For fate had tested their love, and found it strong.

MILLS & BOON®

Makes any time special™

Mills & Boon publish 29 new titles every month. Select from...

Modern Romance™   **Tender Romance**™

Sensual Romance™

Medical Romance™   **Historical Romance**™

MAT2

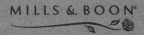